*W*hat the critics are saying...

DRAGON'S TRIBUTE

"This is a very well done paranormal romance with exciting love scenes. But the added element of Rowena having to learn to adapt to dragon ways makes this a very good emotional read...This is a very wonderful and exciting read." ~ *The Romance Studio*

"Dragons and sacrifices, hidden pasts and secrets, this book has all the great aspects of a wonderful story...Great characters and a wonderful plot make *Dragon's Tribute* a real keeper." ~ *Just Erotic Romance Reviews*

VIRGIN BLOOD

"*Virgin Blood* is a hot read that moves along very quickly." ~ *Sensual Romance Reviews*

"Margaret Carter spins a new and fascinating version to the classic Rapunzel tale with *Virgin Blood*. *Virgin Blood* is a steamy and erotic tale that is a fast read, enticing and very enjoyable." ~ *The Road to Romance*

Margaret L. Carter

ELLORA'S CAVE
ROMANTICA PUBLISHING

An Ellora's Cave Romantica Publication

www.ellorascave.com

Maiden Flights

ISBN # 1419952595
ALL RIGHTS RESERVED.
Virgin Blood Copyright© 2003 Margaret Carter
Dragon's Tribute Copyright© 2003 Margaret Carter
Edited by Jennifer Martin and Pamela Campbell
Cover art by Christine Clavel

Trade paperback Publication September 2005

Warning:

The following material contains graphic sexual content meant for mature readers. *Maiden Flights* has been rated *X-treme* by a minimum of three independent reviewers.

Ellora's Cave Publishing offers three levels of Romantica™ reading entertainment: S (S-ensuous), E (E-rotic), and X (X-treme).

S-*ensuous* love scenes are explicit and leave nothing to the imagination.

E-*rotic* love scenes are explicit, leave nothing to the imagination, and are high in volume per the overall word count. In addition, some E-rated titles might contain fantasy material that some readers find objectionable, such as bondage, submission, same sex encounters, forced seductions, etc. E-rated titles are the most graphic titles we carry; it is common, for instance, for an author to use words such as "fucking", "cock", "pussy", etc., within their work of literature.

X-*treme* titles differ from E-rated titles only in plot premise and storyline execution. Unlike E-rated titles, stories designated with the letter X tend to contain controversial subject matter not for the faint of heart.

Also by Margaret L. Carter

ஐ

New Flame

Night Flight

Thing That Go Bump In The Night II *(anthology)*

About the Author

ஐ

Marked for life by reading DRACULA at the age of twelve, Margaret L. Carter specializes in the literature of fantasy and the supernatural, particularly vampires. She received degrees in English from the College of William and Mary, the University of Hawaii, and the University of California. She is a 2000 Eppie Award winner in horror, and with her husband, retired Navy Captain Leslie Roy Carter, she coauthored a fantasy novel, WILD SORCERESS.

Margaret welcomes comments from readers. You can find her website and email address on her author bio page at www.elloracave.com.

Contents

Virgin Blood

ဇာ

Chapter One

ಐ

When the moon rose above the trees, she leaned out the open window to await the call. After answering that summons at every full and new moon in the five years since her monthly flow began, she fell into the pattern automatically.

As always, Mother Selene's voice floated up to the window. "Rapunzel, Rapunzel, let down your hair."

Nude except for her loose gown of white silk, Rapunzel ran her fingers through her waist-length, honey-blonde hair and let the tresses flow over the windowsill. Mother Selene spoke one of the arcane words that instantly evaporated from Rapunzel's mind, syllables only a mage's thoughts could grasp. Ripples of energy coursed through her and pierced her scalp like fingernails probing her skull. The hair blossomed into a net of shimmering gold that spread over the stone walls of the tower from the bedchamber window all the way to the ground. Vibrations tingled along the strands. The witch swarmed up the net like a spider ascending a web.

None of this magic alarmed Rapunzel or even interested her very much. She had seen it too often. Having no gift for magecraft herself, or so Mother Selene assured her, she accepted her role as handmaiden to her guardian. Once inside the chamber, Mother Selene muttered a second word, which restored Rapunzel's hair to its ordinary state. Silently, the witch led the way up the spiral staircase to the roof of the tower.

The circular platform at the top, surrounded by a wall of about waist height, had a pentagram painted on the floor, with symbols inside the star that made Rapunzel's eyes blur if she stared too steadily at them. Needing no direction, she took her place at one point of the diagram, while Mother Selene stepped into position opposite her. The witch, robed in crimson, wore her ceremonial silver athame in a cincture at her waist. Her pale hair grew luxuriantly to her shoulders, with her unlined face giving no clue to her age. Her eyes looked as cold as shards of blue ice. Her appearance had not changed since Rapunzel's earliest memories.

A cool night wind swirled around Rapunzel's bare feet and rustled her gown. Shivers ran up her arms and legs. Mother Selene drew the silver dagger and extended it over the circle inscribed in the center of the pentagram. Rapunzel stretched out her right arm, baring her wrist. The dagger's point nicked the skin. A few drops of blood fell on the circle.

The witch chanted the words, whisked away from Rapunzel's thoughts the moment they touched her ears. At once the familiar sparks danced over her body, encircling both her and her guardian in a blue-green aura. The magic tugged at the roots of her veins and nerves. Her skin prickled, and her hair fanned behind her as if swept by an otherworldly wind. Her nipples hardened, rubbing against the fabric of her robe. She resisted the impulse to clasp her hands to her breasts.

Behind the rhythm of the witch's voice, a clear chime like silver on crystal echoed through the drone of the chanting. Rapunzel felt an icy needle pierce her chest. A shudder racked her. She had never sensed any such interruption to the ritual before.

Mother Selene broke off as if she, too, had felt the intrusion. Shaking her head, though, she immediately resumed the incantation.

The circle on the floor glowed blue. It melted from stone to the rippling surface of a pool. Along with the witch,

Rapunzel gazed into its depths. As usual, she saw nothing but the reflection of starlight and moonlight. Mother Selene whispered questions in an unknown language and paused as if waiting for answers. Whatever answers she saw in the pool of light seemed to please her. At last a cascade of azure light fountained from the pool to flow up her outstretched arms and over her body. The witch purred as if the light caressed her. Rapunzel felt herself floating in dreamy languor. She seemed to drift among the stars like a leaf blown from its twig. She had no idea how much time passed before Mother Selene touched her shoulder to recall her to awareness.

The "pool" had reverted to a lifeless pattern on stone. Mother Selene murmured a phrase that stopped the bleeding from Rapunzel's wrist. "Well done, my child. Come along."

They descended the stairs to the bedchamber. Looking out the window, Rapunzel saw two covered baskets, each attached to a coil of rope. The witch spoke her magical summons, and each rope, in turn, floated up to the window to be reeled in. Rapunzel didn't hurry to rummage through the baskets, since she knew they contained the usual fresh fruits, bread, and other necessities to supply her for the coming fortnight.

"Is there anything else you'd like me to bring next time, dear?" Mother Selene asked with her chilly smile. "New books or music?"

Rapunzel glanced at her harp in the corner. She still hadn't finished mastering the last folio of sheet music. "No, thank you. I'm content." By now she knew it would be useless to ask for her real wants. *Teach me some of your magic.* Or, *I want to leave this tower and explore the world.*

Mother Selene didn't linger. It had been years since she had made any pretense that she and her ward got pleasure from each other's company. Still, as Rapunzel fetched the empty baskets from the previous visit, she almost wished she could think of a topic to detain her guardian for a few minutes. Talking to the witch would be more interesting than talking to herself or the sparrows she sometime lured to the window with crumbs.

After giving her a cool kiss on the cheek, Mother Selene spoke the words that transformed Rapunzel's hair once again into a shimmering net of gold. She descended to the ground, reversed the magic, and got into her waiting carriage, drawn by a single horse. A word of command, with no need for a hand on the reins, spurred the animal into motion. Rapunzel watched until the carriage disappeared into the woods.

Tired from her role in the ceremony, even though it drained only a few drops of her blood, she hung her ritual gown in the wardrobe and lay down, naked, on the bed. The breeze from the open window caressed her flesh, still warm from the magical energies. Her palms grazed her nipples, then stroked down over her chest and stomach to her thighs. Heat pooled between her legs. She let her eyes drift shut.

Abruptly a voice broke into her half-dreaming state. "Rapunzel, Rapunzel!"

Her eyes snapped open. "Mother Selene?" No, the witch would have no reason to return. And the voice was a stranger's. A deep voice that reverberated through Rapunzel like the peal of a huge bell.

"Who's there?" she whispered. No one else ever came near the tower.

The voice called her again. "Rapunzel, Rapunzel, answer me!"

She snatched her dressing gown from a chair by the bed and shrugged into it. She rushed to the window and looked down.

A tall, cloaked figure stood there, taller even than the witch, who towered over Rapunzel. It pushed back the hood of the cloak and stared up at her. Its eyes gleamed in the moonlight.

A man!

He flashed a smile. "Lovely Rapunzel, let me come up to you."

"How do you know my name?" she called down.

"I overheard the witch speaking to you. May I come up?"

She wrapped her arms around herself. "You can't, unless you have magic like hers. Do you?"

"Not exactly, but I can reach your window if you're willing. You have to invite me."

Mother Selene's warnings raced through her mind. The outside world was not safe for young women. Rapunzel was cloistered here for her own protection. Men, especially, were little more than wild beasts on two legs. On the other side of the question, a flutter in the pit of Rapunzel's stomach argued in the man's favor. She told herself the excitement came from meeting someone new after all this time. She would risk any number of phantom hazards for a few hours of conversation with this stranger.

"Very well, I invite you. Come in."

The man spread his cloak. It swirled around him like a windblown cloud. A second later, it shrank inward, and his body with it. Human limbs became wings. A huge, ghost-white owl soared up and flew in circles just outside the window.

Rapunzel's breath caught in her throat. She backed away, one hand pressed to her mouth, the other to her pounding heart. The bird swooped in through the open shutters. It expanded to a column of dark mist, then shifted to man-shape.

Margaret L. Carter

She backed up farther and collapsed onto the bed, where she sat, gaping at him. He unfastened his cloak and flung it aside. With an amused arch of his black eyebrows, he said, "Have you never seen a man before?"

The faint mockery in his tone replaced some of her alarm with indignation. "Of course I have, when I was a child. But they were servants and tradesmen. None of them changed into birds."

Taking a seat in the bedside chair, he stretched his legs out and folded his arms. "You haven't always lived in this tower, then?"

"No, Mother Selene brought me here when I was thirteen." *When I became a woman.* "Before that, we lived in her mansion in the city." She surveyed her visitor. He wore black trousers with a lace-trimmed, white shirt, open at the neck. His dark hair curled in waves to just below his ears. His face, in contrast, was as marble-pale as the witch's. His eyes glowed in the darkness of the bedroom, with a glint of crimson at their centers. "Are you a wizard?" she asked.

"As I said, not exactly."

"Then what brings you here?"

"You did, lovely Rapunzel. I was traveling through the forest, and your blood called to me. Your sweet, virgin blood. Like silver chimes ringing in my head."

She felt a stiletto of ice pierce her heart, just as she had during the ritual. Was it too late to eject this stranger from her refuge? Shivers danced over her body, and her nipples peaked again. "What do you mean?" she whispered.

"I'm no magician, not in the way you understand, but I can't help sensing the power of blood magic. And the fragrance of your blood ravished me."

16

"Blood magic." Rapunzel shook her head in bewilderment. "Yes, Mother Selene uses my blood in her ceremonies. But I never knew it was so powerful."

"Doubtless you are very valuable to her. Is she really your mother?"

"No, my parents didn't want me. They sold me to her when I was a baby."

"Or so she told you."

The skepticism in his voice irritated her. "She gives me everything I could possibly need. My real parents were poor. They could never have given me all this. Why should I doubt her goodness?"

He spread his hands to indicate the chamber walls. "She keeps you locked in this tower, doesn't she?"

"For my own protection." She frowned to hear the stranger echo the thoughts she had tried so often to suppress. "The outside world isn't safe for maidens."

"What hazards does she claim to protect you from?" The man stepped to the bedside and loomed over her. "Hazards like me?"

"Men." Rapunzel clutched her robe shut at the neckline. His voice made knots in her stomach, and his eyes glowed hotter the closer he crept. "She's guarding me from men."

He laughed softly. "She's guarding your precious maidenhead. Without your virginity, your blood would become useless for the rituals. But not for me." His cool fingers brushed her hair back from her forehead. She flinched. "Don't be afraid, golden Rapunzel. Haven't you wondered exactly what this danger from men consists of?"

Almost against her will, she nodded. When he smoothed her hair again, her insides churned. "You're no ordinary man," she whispered.

"No." He smiled broader than he had before, showing teeth that gleamed with the sharpness of a wolf's. "But I can demonstrate those *dangers* for you, and more besides."

"What do you want?" Her voice quavered.

He bent over her to flick her earlobe with his tongue. "To taste you. To sip your nectar."

Though she had no idea what he meant, the words roused a flutter inside her that held more delight than fear. "Will it hurt?"

"Oh, no. Does this hurt?" He pried her fingers loose from the robe and folded it open, then trailed one finger down the hollow of her throat to the spot between her breasts.

Her skin tingled, and her nipples tightened. "No," she breathed.

"This?" He ran his fingers through her hair, swept it up from her shoulders, and kissed the nape of her neck. Chills cascaded down her spine. "Or this?" His lips nibbled a path along her jawline to her mouth.

She gasped, and he captured her open mouth with his own. His tongue invaded her to explore the inside of her lips. She extended her own tongue to sample the hot tip of his. Skimming his teeth, she felt a momentary sting. "Oh!" She pulled back.

The crimson glow of his eyes impaled her. "Just as I expected. You taste intoxicating. May I continue the demonstration?"

She trembled at the sight of those teeth that could probably rip her open in one quick bite. The coil of heat in the center of her body, though, made her reckless. "I don't even know your name." Even while she protested, she let the robe fall open and reclined on the pillow.

"Call me Alaric." He swept his palms over her shoulders and down to her breasts, which already ached. She moaned when his hands skipped lightly over her bosom to her waist, then up again without lingering. Grabbing his wrists, she tried to pull his hands from her shoulders back to her breasts. He chuckled. "In time, my love."

He leaned over her and sampled her lips again. Her tongue probed, inviting his to thrust deeper into her mouth. Trapping her legs under one of his, Alaric cupped her left breast and teased the nipple with his thumb. An almost unbearable tingling spread from that spot to the opposite nipple, then over her whole body.

"Alaric, please!" she murmured against the burning of his lips.

"If you beg that way," he growled into the curve of her neck, "you'll make me too thirsty to wait."

"Wait for what?" Hot liquid pooled between her thighs. She felt an urge to arch her hips, but his leg held her prisoner.

"You'll see. Soon." His tongue flickered like a flame across her throat, down the center of her chest, and over to one taut peak. When the wet tip swirled around the nipple, she cried out and writhed under him. While he licked that breast, he fondled the other, letting his palm graze its nipple just enough to drive her into delirium.

"More, please!" She hardly knew what she wanted, except that the tender place between her legs throbbed more urgently than it ever had after the moon magic.

Alaric rose up, evoking a cry of protest from her when the night air wafted over her bare flesh. He tore off his shirt and lay across her. "I need to feel your heat on my skin," he said before his mouth seized hers once more. Her breasts ached and tingled even more intensely, squeezed against his hard, cool chest.

His hand crept down the front of her body. When it reached the curls at the apex of her legs, fresh heat welled up there. She spread her thighs, moaning desperate pleas into his mouth. He dipped into her wetness. She gasped at the sensation of his fingers stroking back and forth between the pulsing folds. Not even in the restless dreams that often followed the rituals had she felt such a thrill.

His mouth traveled from hers to her throat. She felt a sting there, but it didn't feel like pain. Instead, it shot from her neck through her breasts all the way down, making her quiver with more intense need. The tiny nubbin between her thighs twitched. Somehow Alaric seemed to sense its ache. His thumb skimmed over it, making Rapunzel arch her hips in wordless pleading. Whimpers escaped from her lips as he rubbed the swelling bud. It thickened, tingled, and vibrated. Her senses gathered to a single, fiery point at that spot. She convulsed, almost shaking Alaric off her, but still dimly aware of his mouth fastened to her throat. Her whole being seemed to flow into him at the moment of ecstasy.

Drained, shaking, she clung to him until he raised his head to gaze down at her. In the moonlight she glimpsed dark moisture around his mouth. He licked it away with a catlike swirl of his tongue.

"My blood," she whispered. "You drank my blood."

"I told you it called me. And it is sweeter than I even imagined." He stroked her hair. "And it didn't hurt, did it?"

"Oh, no," she sighed. "Is that the whole danger my guardian warned me about?"

He laughed. "That is only the beginning. May I visit tomorrow night for another demonstration?" He stood up to shrug into his shirt and draped the cloak around his shoulders.

Rapunzel braced herself on one elbow, hardly able to gather the energy to move that far. "Not until tomorrow?"

"You need rest, my sweet." He kissed her on the forehead. "Until tomorrow night." He wrapped the cloak around himself, contracted to a swirl of black fog, transformed into bird shape, and flew out the window.

Rapunzel lay back with a shuddering sigh and drifted into sleep.

Chapter Two

ஐ

The next day she wondered whether the whole visit had been a dream. The tangled sheets hinted otherwise, though, and when she looked into the mirror, she saw a tiny scratch on her neck. She rubbed the wound. It felt faintly sore but didn't really hurt. In fact, touching it stirred a tickle between her legs. Blushing at the memories that flooded her with that sensation, she hurried downstairs, past her parlor and dining nook, to the lowest level of the tower.

There, a garden of shrubs and flowers, designed to bloom through most of the year, grew in the sunlight that shone through the lattice-covered windows. A well supplied all the water Rapunzel needed. As on every other morning, she used the bucket to scoop water into a tub beside the well. Magic infused in the construction of the tub caused it to warm the water to the precise temperature comfortable for her bath. Sometime after she'd finished (she never saw the process) the used water vanished. The same kind of magic kept dishes, floors, and clothes clean, emptied her chamber pot, and, in winter, disposed of ashes from the fireplaces.

Sometimes she wished the magic didn't make all dirt vanish without a human touch. She had little enough to occupy her time as it was. After bathing and dressing, she ascended to the second level. Here, too, latticework covered the windows. In the past she had accepted Mother Selene's explanation that the barriers guarded against forest-dwelling outlaws who might try to break in. Now it dawned on Rapunzel that the lattice also served to keep her from running away. She had never thought of her doorless tower as a prison before. Now its solitude seemed just that, rather than the refuge she had always been taught to call it.

She lit a fire to boil water for tea and porridge, one task the magic didn't perform. After breakfast, consisting of the porridge and a peach from the basket delivered the night before, she wandered around the room taking books off the shelves, opening and closing them, unable to settle down. The pictures, in colors brighter than life, moved when she focused on them. Usually, the miniature scenes kept her entertained for hours. Today, though, even a sea monster sinking a ship in one of the newest books failed to hold her attention. She picked up her embroidery, only to prick her finger and narrowly escape dripping blood on the white linen. Sucking the needle wound, she remembered Alaric's mouth at her throat and blushed hotly.

At last she walked up to the third floor, her bedchamber, and tried to distract herself with the harp. Only love ballads flowed from her mind through her hands to the strings. She got up from the harp, shaking her head at her own infatuation. She might as well be one of those imprisoned princesses in the tales, mooning around while waiting for her prince to rescue her. Would Alaric be the prince to carry her off to freedom?

How could he? His magic of transformation into a bird wouldn't let her fly away, too.

She gazed out the window over the unbroken sea of green treetops that faded into mist at the horizon. Where had he come from? Where had he gone for the day? Could he find shelter in that untamed forest?

* * * * *

When night fell, she lit a single lamp on the bedside table and stared out that same window. The moon, waning from full, cast its pale light on the clearing at the foot of the tower.

She hadn't long to wait before Alaric's darkly cloaked figure stepped out of the woods.

"Rapunzel, let me in!"

"Yes, hurry, come up!" The sound of his voice chased away her shame and annoyance with herself for yearning after him all day. Joy at his return erased all doubts. A delicious shiver coursed over her body while she watched him change size and shift into owl form.

The bird soared to the window and swooped inside. He had scarcely solidified into man shape before she threw herself into his arms. "You promised more," she murmured into the lace of his shirt. "Show me."

His chest vibrated with something between a laugh and a purr. "All in time, my golden one." His hands swept from her hair down her back to the curve of her hips, over and over, until she rubbed against him like a cat.

After a pause to shed his cloak and unfasten his shirt, he clasped her tightly and nuzzled her throat. "For the demonstration I promised, I have to taste your elixir first." Opening her loose robe, he hugged her so that she felt his cool skin against the heat of her breasts. Her nipples pebbled up. He insinuated one hand inside her robe and reached around to fondle her cleft from behind.

With a moan of impatience, she arched against him. His fingers crept between her legs. "Let me into your secret grotto."

"Yes, please!" She spread her thighs to invite a deeper probe.

"Like the dew of a summer night," he whispered. His tongue flickered over her neck.

Already she throbbed inside. When he stopped working at her slit, she whimpered in protest, but his hand quickly shifted to the front. The long middle fingers danced in and out of her eager flesh, while his thumb slid over the sensitive bud in the nest of hair.

"Ah," he sighed. "I feel your pearl glistening at my touch."

She rocked back and forth to the rhythm of his strokes. The tension grew to an unbearable tightness, aching to explode in release. Her whole body pulsed in tune with her heartbeat.

"I can hear your heart," he echoed her thoughts. "It intoxicates me." His teeth penetrated her throat. Her blood and her passion erupted together.

She clung to him, shaking, with only his arms holding her upright. When their ecstasy began to fade, he carried her to the bed. "Now that your essence fills me, I can perform the rest of the demonstration."

After stripping her of the robe, he peeled off his own shirt and trousers. She watched him in wonder. Between his thighs jutted a long column of flesh that tapered to a point. She reached out, daring to touch it with a fingertip. The strange organ twitched at the contact.

"As I said, I'm no wizard in the sense you understand." Alaric reclined next to her. "But I do have a rod of enchantment."

She tilted her head back to look into his teasing eyes. "Can you really work magic?"

He laughed. "Only the magic all lovers share."

"Then what is the purpose of this, this rod?" Again she gave it a tentative poke.

Growling, he caught her hand. "Not so fast. To cast the spell, it must enter your grotto, if you'll allow me."

At those words, a fresh gush of hot wetness pooled in her "grotto." Yet his rod looked so large. "Will it hurt?"

"I would never cause you pain." Easing her onto her back, he swept his hands from her shoulders over her breasts and stomach, down the insides of her legs, then upward in long, swirling strokes that made every inch of skin glow with heat. She felt herself melting, even though her inner muscles tightened with each pass of his hands. "Touch me now," he invited.

She clasped his rod. The shaft felt like ivory covered with satin. With a groan, he thrust into her grasp. "Now," he said, "let my rod into your sheath."

He knelt between her spread legs. Her hole pulsed with eagerness. In a single plunge, he buried himself to the hilt inside her. Still melting from his caresses, she felt no pain, only fullness. He rocked his hips, and she matched the rhythm. He withdrew almost completely. With a moan of protest, she arched her back to draw him deeper again. He glided in and out, tantalizing her passion-swollen button with each long, slow stroke. Molten heat spread from that spot to flow throughout her body.

Their pace quickened, until the frantic thrusting drove her to the heights again. Quivering on the verge, she clamped her legs around him. Her inner muscles clenched and throbbed while he spurted into her. Just as she began to slide down from that peak, she felt his teeth in her throat. The sting spurred her to yet another release.

Over and over, she spiraled higher and higher with him, scarcely pausing to catch breath before he made her soar again. When the time came for him to fly away, she had to clutch him to keep her tremulous legs from collapsing under her.

"Perhaps I've drunk too deeply. I should stay away for awhile."

"No, don't do that!"

"I can't risk being caught by the witch. There's no telling what she would do to you if she learned about our lovemaking."

"It's all right," Rapunzel said, still breathless in the aftermath of her satisfaction. "She won't—she doesn't come here every night. Only twice a month. Tomorrow is safe."

They shared a ravenous kiss before he shifted shape and left her just ahead of the dawn.

Chapter Three

ॐ

Even before Alaric called to her the next evening, she saw his dark figure at the foot of the tower and begged him to come up. When he alighted in front of her and blurred from owl-shape to man-shape, she wrapped her arms around him and tugged him toward the bed.

Laughing softly, he drew her onto his lap. "Rapunzel, would you like me to show you a new kind of danger?"

She giggled. "Do you mean a new pleasure?"

He nuzzled her neck. "You've changed your mind fast enough about the witch's view of men."

A shadow fell across Rapunzel's delight. "Let's not talk about her. What is this new pleasure, or danger?"

"I want to prepare you first, if I may." He caressed the nape of her neck under her unbound hair.

Sighing, she leaned her head back against his hand. "How?"

"Let's begin by removing your clothes."

Her skin tingled at the words. Since she wore only a long nightgown, that preparation would be easy. She reached for the ribbons at her neck.

"Allow me." He pulled the first bow loose. His cool fingers made her flesh prickle. He followed up with a light kiss on the exposed hollow of her throat.

She gasped. He untied the second ribbon. His lips brushed her skin just above her breasts. Another ribbon. Now he could fold the bodice of the gown open to expose her nipples. His hands cupped each breast and grazed the hardening peaks.

His mouth followed the path of his hands. When she clutched his arms, he slipped out of her grasp and moved down to slide his hands under the hem that reached to her ankles. Inch by inch, he eased the cloth up to expose her legs. His fingers crept up the inside of her calves, then her thighs. She writhed and arched her hips. When his hand reached the apex of her thighs, he didn't dip into the wet cavity but skimmed over the triangle of hair to fold the gown above her waist.

He planted a kiss on her navel, then pulled the gown the rest of the way over her head. Her impatient squirming almost got her tangled in the cloth.

"Alaric, please! I need—"

"So do I." He ran one fingertip from her throat to her navel. It felt like a searing brand. "Soon." He shrugged off the cloak and unfastened his shirt to pull it off.

Rapunzel tugged at the buttons of his trousers until at last they both lay naked side by side. His rod nudged her mound, but it wasn't completely stiff, and he made no move to enter. "Now I can show you that new pleasure," he said. With one fingernail he slashed a line across his chest. Blood oozed from the scratch. "Taste me." He drew her head toward him.

The excitement bubbling in her veins kept her from feeling repelled at the idea of drinking blood. She kissed each of his nipples in turn, exulting in their hardness and the groan he uttered when her tongue touched them. With his hand on the back of her head guiding her, she licked the thin wound.

His blood tasted like crisp, dry wine. It burned like brandy on her tongue and all the way down to her stomach.

Ripples of pleasure undulated over her body. Her slit pulsed at the pressure of his shaft against her lower abdomen.

"Rapunzel, my golden one—" She felt a growl rumble in his chest. When she sucked on the scratch to stimulate the trickle of blood, he moaned as if transfixed by pain or pleasure. "Rapunzel, give me your hand," he begged in a strangled voice.

She stretched her arm to bring it within his reach. Lifting her hand to his mouth, he bit her wrist and sucked with frantic urgency. His tongue danced over her skin. A lightning bolt seemed to shoot up her arm and down to the pit of her stomach. Wet heat welled inside her.

She felt his rod growing hard. Draping one leg over his, she tried to roll onto her back without removing her mouth from his chest.

"Not yet," he whispered in between sips from her wrist. His other hand crept between their bodies and stroked her damp curls. "Let me polish your pearl first." His fingers circled the thick bud until her hips pumped uncontrollably. Then he found the swollen tip and settled into a steady "polishing" rhythm. After a few seconds the flood of ecstasy swept over her. The piquant flavor of his blood intoxicated her beyond anything she'd felt before.

His hips bucked, rubbing his shaft against her belly. "It needs—relief—now." He broke off their mutual blood-sipping and rolled her over to lie on top. Spreading her legs, she drew his rod into her sheath. He captured her mouth while she convulsed in release, and she tasted her own elixir on his lips.

"What did that mean?" she said when she recovered her breath. "Making me drink your blood?"

He kissed the top of her head. "It's like a marriage. Perhaps I should have told you first, but I couldn't bear the thought that you might refuse."

She leaned on one elbow to gaze into his glowing eyes. "Have you done that with many other girls?"

He laughed softly. "Never. Do you think I'm a polygamist?" He pulled her head onto his shoulder. "That sensation was incredible. I can't imagine having it with anyone but you. Now that you've tasted my blood, we have a special bond. We can share dreams."

"Really? You mean you can get inside my dreams?" She wasn't sure how she felt about such intimacy.

"And I can bestow dreams upon you. Visions as real as life. You can travel with me in your sleep. Wouldn't you like to see what lies beyond this tower?"

"You know I would. It's what I want most." She thought of her fading memories of the outside world from childhood and the moving pictures in her books. Neither one quelled her discontent any longer.

"Then I'll give you what I can of that through our bond until the night comes when you're ready to leave with me."

"Leave?" She hadn't thought that far ahead. Alaric's visits seemed more like a dream than anything that could affect her waking life.

"Did you expect to spend the rest of your life here?"

The question dissipated the languid contentment left from their embrace. She sat up, wrapping her arms around her knees. "Mother Selene has never mentioned that."

"Why don't you ask her next time? I'll wager she'll evade the issue or become angry."

Rapunzel's heart chilled at the thought of making the witch angry. Yet didn't her foster mother owe her the truth about her own future? "I'll think about it."

"Meanwhile, we can travel together in visions. You'll see a bit of what you're missing. Tonight while you're sleeping, perhaps."

"Why not while you're with me?"

"I don't trust myself to break out of the trance in time," he said. "I don't want to be caught by the sun."

After he left, she lay awake until well past midnight, mulling over the doubts he'd stirred in her. Finally she drifted into sleep.

Some unmeasured time later, her eyes opened to find her chamber drenched in moonlight. She had never seen it so bright before, like lamplight, yet without the flickering and the shadows. A pearly glow filled the room.

Rapunzel threw back the sheet and sat up. Abruptly she realized she was not wearing her nightshift, nor was she sitting in a normal position. She seemed to be crouched on her feet. Glancing down at her breast, she saw white feathers. When she tried to stretch her arms, wings flapped instead.

I'm an owl. The idea didn't frighten her. In a dreamy daze, she realized this change must be one of the "visions" Alaric had promised.

She spread her wings and fluttered to the open window. Above the treetops a white bird with glowing eyes flew in wide circles. It swooped toward the window and greeted her with a ghostly "whoo" cry.

Alaric.

His voice spoke inside her head. *Fly with me.*

She stretched to her full wingspan and leaped out the window. A gust of wind caught and lifted her. Gliding on the currents, she followed the other owl over the forest. *Where are we going?*

We shall hunt. He led the way across the expanse of trees to a break in the foliage that showed a clearing far below. Rapunzel exulted in the wind rushing past her and ruffling her feathers. On the ground in the clearing she caught sight of small, pale shapes crawling through the undergrowth.

Every object looked more distinct than the waning moon could account for, as if her owl form could use even the faintest glimmers of light.

Alaric spiraled downward, and she followed. When she got closer to the earth, her eyes picked out each leaf and blade of grass. She recognized the creatures on the ground as field mice. Their squeaks of alarm pierced her ears. Her stomach cramped with hunger.

Watch. Alaric's circles tightened as he descended. He centered on one mouse in the middle of the clearing. In a steep dive he rushed down to snatch the animal in his talons. His beak stabbed the back of its neck. The tiny body went limp. The owl pecked a deeper wound in its belly and, instead of tearing it apart, sipped the blood.

Rapunzel chose her own target and dove toward it. The mice scattered in panic, and her strike missed. She pulled up with a screech of frustration.

Leaving his drained prey, Alaric flew up to join her. *The forest is full of game. We'll find your food elsewhere.*

They soared over the woods again. Rapunzel noticed isolated clusters of lights that suggested villages. In the distance sparkled larger clumps of light that could be towns or cities. Why hadn't she ever seen them from her tower window? On the other hand, it made sense that a dream landscape might not match the reality she knew.

Flying over the trees, she glimpsed deer and foxes, all too large for her to attack. Alaric led her to another clearing, where a family of rabbits crouched asleep under a bush. Her keen vision noted when their eyes opened and their ears perked up. Alaric dove toward them with a screech that frightened them into running. Rapunzel focused on one fleeing rabbit and flew straight at it. Her claws sank into the fur. It squealed in terror, and its muscles flexed in her grip.

She plucked the animal off the ground, circled the clearing, landed again, and drove her beak into the victim's spine.

Beside her, Alaric also had a catch in his talons. She watched him stab the other rabbit and feed on its blood. Encouraged, she impaled her own prey and tasted the red fluid that gushed from the wound. It filled and intoxicated her like a rich wine. She drank until the flow subsided to a trickle. Her stomach felt pleasantly heavy with its warmth.

They launched into the air, flying on the wind for what felt like hours. She marveled at the brightness of the gibbous moon and the diamond sharpness of the stars. Finally they circled back toward the tower. Her wings still bore her weight with no fatigue. She almost wished she could do this every night.

Alaric must have picked up the thought, for he answered, *Vision flights take their toll on your strength, even if you don't feel it at present. Tomorrow you will need a long rest to recover.*

She flew around the tower in playful retreat, and he chased her. Catching up, he paced her so that his wings barely grazed hers. The brush of his feathers stirred an appetite for more than food or drink. Heat coiled in her loins. Alighting on the edge of the roof, she flapped her wings invitingly. He swooped down upon her.

Overshadowing her, he mounted her back. His beak grasped her neck, and he pressed against the opening beneath her tail. His wings beat the air, whipping up a wind that made her feathers bristle. A thrill rippled through her. She humped in time with his frenzied rubbing. When their release exploded together, both of them shrieked aloud.

Alaric nipped her gently in farewell and flew away. She glided to her window and hopped inside. The moment she landed on the floor, oblivion took her.

* * * * *

When she lay in his arms after their lovemaking the next time he visited, she described her dream. "But you know all about it, don't you? You were with me."

"Yes, in a way."

She rolled on her stomach and propped her chin on her fists to stare into his eyes. "Now you sound like Mother Selene. She never gives a straight answer about magic, either."

"I told you, I don't perform magic the same way she does."

"I know you're not a wizard," Rapunzel said. "If you were, you could cast a spell to whisk me away from here when I'm awake, not only in dreams. If you aren't a wizard, though, how do you work that dream magic?"

"It is part of what I am." He turned on his side and leaned on one elbow. "I didn't have to learn it as an apprentice or from books. I gained the ability when I became a creature of the night, like the power to fly in owl shape."

"You mean you haven't always been like this?"

He laughed. "Of course not. Do you think I'm some sort of demon? I used to be as human as you are."

"Then what happened?"

"I have to delve far into my memory to recall that. It was a very long time ago. Hundreds of years."

Her heart constricted. "How is that possible? You're young. You don't look much older than I do."

"The change stopped me from aging. Dear one, I died all those centuries ago."

Her heart congealed into a cold knot. She sat up and gazed at the candle glowing on the bedside table. "You can't be dead."

"I said I died," came his gentle reply. "I didn't stay dead." His fingers played with her unbound hair.

Shrugging off his touch, she said, "Tell me about it."

"I was a younger son of a minor lord. I've since learned that most revenants who survive long after their return from the grave are noble or at least wealthy."

"Why?"

"Because serfs and peasants can't pay for adequate shelter and protection. It's all too easy for their neighbors to unearth and destroy them."

Rapunzel felt sickened at the thought of anything hurting Alaric. "Destroy—how?"

"A wooden stake or silver weapon in the heart. Cutting off the head. Or the surest method, fire." He patted her hand. "Don't distress yourself. Nothing will happen to me. I've managed to survive all this time."

The coolness of his skin reminded her of his claim to have died. Moving her hand away, she said, "How does a person become one of the living dead? A curse from a sorcerer or a demon?"

"Possibly. I'm no scholar, to answer such questions. The commonest way is through the bite of another revenant."

"You mean I—"

"Only if you die of my feeding, or of any cause while the wounds remain unhealed."

"One of the living dead changed you, then?"

He got up and strode to the window, where he stared out at the moon. "My father gave a Christmas feast for the nobility and gentry of the district. A woman with flame-colored hair and milk-white skin appeared in the ballroom after dinner. No one knew her name or remembered seeing her before, yet my parents and older brothers made no move to challenge her. She behaved as if she had a right to walk among us. And she chose me as her partner in the dance."

"Chose you? Didn't you have any say in the matter?"

"It seemed not," he said with a wry smile. "One moment she was standing in front of me, gazing into my eyes. The next, I was leading her in time to the musicians' measure. I felt drunk, as if my head floated apart from my body. The woman was as thin as a wraith, but though I normally preferred buxom ladies, I didn't find her unappealing. Quite the opposite. Every moment the pattern of the dance moved her out of my reach, I felt shrouded in darkness. She enthralled me."

Rapunzel's queasiness gave way to annoyance. "Enough of that. Never mind how thrilling she was. What happened next?"

He gave her a teasing smile. "Oh, you don't want to hear how I followed the stranger around like a lovesick boy for the rest of the night? Or how I escorted her to the sideboard, but she would accept nothing from me but a goblet of wine, which I never saw her drink? When the ball finally ended, I strolled outside with her and ordered a servant to summon her carriage. I looked around for my strange lady, and she was gone."

"You mean she vanished into thin air?"

"Not literally before my eyes, but she might as well have. I searched frantically and couldn't find her, nor did anyone remember seeing her leave. And I still didn't know her name."

"It's like an old tale," said Rapunzel. "She didn't drop a crystal slipper on the stairs, did she?"

He laughed. "No, but like the prince in the tale, I scoured the town and countryside for my mysterious beauty. None of my father's guests knew her or admitted inviting her. After two days of futile questioning, I gave up. On the third night, she visited me."

"I suspect you don't mean she arrived in a coach with footmen."

Alaric shook his head. "She came to me in a dream. At least, I thought it was a dream. She appeared in my bedchamber wearing the same forest green velvet dress she had worn at the ball. But her copper hair flowed loose instead of being elegantly coifed the way it had been when I'd danced with her. I tried to sit up, to speak. I couldn't move, as if I was chained to the bed and gagged."

"Could you have done that to me?" For the first time since the night they'd met, Rapunzel thought of him as a creature to be feared.

"I could, but I wouldn't. I wanted your free consent." The warmth in his voice sounded sincere.

"I'm glad."

"She glided to my bedside. Somehow her clothes melted away, leaving her white body naked in the moonlight. She turned down the covers and lay on top of me." His voice softened into a dreamy, distant tone. "She felt like ice, drawing the life out of me. But her lips burned my neck. A sting at my throat sent the most exquisite convulsion of pain and pleasure through—" He shook his head as if forcing himself back to the present. "Well, you don't need to hear that part. Hours seemed to pass, hours of passion that would have been impossible in waking life. Finally blackness closed over me."

"You mean she killed you?" She wasn't sure which disturbed her more to hear about, the woman's seducing him or murdering him.

He blinked. "What? No, not then. She wanted to prolong the enjoyment. I woke the next morning parched with thirst and so weak I could hardly stand. Food and drink revived me, though, and by evening I felt almost like myself. That night the 'dream' came again. I luxuriated in her embrace. After all, if it was only a phantom of my fevered brain, it couldn't be sinful."

"Did you think it might be?" Though Rapunzel had read about the rituals of the church, Mother Selene had, of course, never had her christened or instructed in religion.

With a bleak smile, he said, "Our local priest would certainly have said so. Consorting with a demon, for what else could she be, if she were real? By daylight I assured myself I'd only dreamed her visits, so I didn't have to settle the question of her nature."

"And by night?" Again she felt a prickle of jealousy over his fascination with the strange woman.

He sighed. "Her passion proved tireless, and under her spell, I kept pace with her—by night. During the day was a different matter. Before too long, though, my family couldn't help noticing my fatigue and loss of appetite. They called physicians, who bled me—for all the good that did on top of her feedings—and dosed me with foul potions. My health kept fading."

"Surely you must have known she'd caused the illness."

"No, she fogged my brain so that I didn't realize she was drinking from me. Anyway, as I said, I told myself she was only a dream. Finally my father gave up on physicians and summoned the priest. He prayed over me day after day. He heard my confession and brought me the Host daily, and at last I broke down and confessed my lustful dreams. He ordered me to recite hours of rosaries as penance and wear a crucifix to sleep."

"That didn't keep her away, did it?" By now Rapunzel knew how the story had to end.

He sighed. "It might have if my own will hadn't undermined its power. When she appeared that night, she saw the cross around my neck and bared her fangs in rage. The next moment, she cooed with honey sweetness again and asked with tears in her eyes if I'd ceased to love her. I protested my devotion. Then she said I had to prove it by taking off the cross. I'm sure it won't surprise you that I obeyed her."

Tingling at the memory of the passion Alaric always roused in her, Rapunzel could hardly blame him for responding the same way to his long-ago lover.

"Still assuring myself that she wasn't real, I discarded the holy symbol and embraced her. She must have grown tired of me, or perhaps she didn't want the risk of being unmasked, maybe even destroyed, by the priest. This time she fed deeply and didn't bother to conceal the wound. I woke up the next morning too weak to move, with my pillow soaked in blood."

Rapunzel's stomach churned. "And then you—died?"

He nodded. "Though I didn't know it, of course. I received the last rites and fell into a swoon a few hours later. I woke in the dark. In a box." A visible shudder went through him.

She moved from the bed to stand beside him, putting her arm around his waist.

He drew her close. "Don't upset yourself, dear one. It was a very long time ago."

"But it must have been horrible."

"As I said, I didn't know I had died, only that I was trapped in a wooden chest. I screamed myself hoarse and kicked the sides and pounded the lid. My fists punched holes in the wood, and I tore at it until I'd made a gap large enough to escape through. That alone should have told me I had changed. No ordinary human strength could have broken out."

"Were you buried?" She forced out the words in a thready whisper.

"My family had a crypt. I recognized my surroundings as soon as my panic wore down to mere terror. Naturally, I thought I'd been entombed alive. I shouted for help, though with little hope that anyone would be close enough to hear. Then the door opened."

"Someone from your family freed you?"

"Hardly," he said with a dry laugh. "It was my lady. Her eyes glittered with contempt instead of passion. She explained what I'd become and told me to be grateful she'd stayed long enough to watch me rise, rather than abandoning me. She said she'd already waited longer than she planned and had almost lost patience. You see, the time for resurrection varies from mere hours to several nights, for reasons unknown to me."

"So she stayed to help you?"

"She gave little enough help. She had no interest in her victims once they couldn't nourish her anymore. After she'd introduced me to the rudiments of this existence, she considered her duty finished. After all, why should she linger in the area and risk destruction for one more half-witted boy, as she put it?"

"How cruel!" The bitterness in his tone brought tears to Rapunzel's eyes.

"Don't be afraid, my love." He stroked her cheek. "If you ever become what I am, I won't let you suffer any such fate."

She leaned against him. "You must have dallied with many women over the years."

"Not this way. I visited them in dreams, and only two or three times each. I vowed I wouldn't treat any woman the way my dream lady ravished and abandoned me. To the end, I never even knew her name."

"What did you do when she left you? Go back to your family?"

"I knew better than that. They would have received me with sword, stake, and fire. By night I slipped into my old chambers to collect money and gems. They belonged to me, after all. It wasn't theft. I traveled far from home and finally settled near your forest. While hunting one night, I sensed the call of your blood."

She tilted her head back to gaze up at him. "That explains why you visited me the first time. Why have you kept returning? And why didn't you make me believe you're a dream?"

He rubbed her back in languid spirals. "Do I need a reason to fall in love with you?"

"Yes. Why me? I'm an ordinary girl."

Laughing, he kissed the top of her head. "Far from it! The witch has guarded you like a jewel in a golden casket. Because of your innocence, you welcomed me without fear. Few other women could do that. It was an entirely new experience for me, to feast on your love in full waking awareness. It enthralled me from the first time we embraced." His tone became more somber. "Now that you know the truth of my past, do you fear me?"

"Oh, no!" She wrapped her arms around him. "I love you."

"Dearest. My golden one." His voice sounded rough with suppressed tears. He bent to kiss her, cradling the back of her head in his palm. His tongue teased her lips apart.

Sighing, she welcomed the penetration and pressed her body tight against the full length of his. Liquid heat flowed through her. She stood on tiptoe to let his hardness nestle in the V of her hips.

With a shaky laugh, he broke off the kiss. "No more of that. Dawn grows near." He placed his open palm over her racing heart. "Rapunzel, sooner or later you'll escape from this prison. I promise that. And when you do, you'll meet other people. Men and women like yourself, ordinary, as you put it. You want that, don't you?"

"Of course. I remember a little of what it was like to talk to people besides Mother Selene. I'd love to be able to do that again and travel freely outside my own rooms. Even when we lived in the city, I couldn't do that. She didn't trust me out of her sight, even with my nursemaid. On our rare excursions beyond the walls of the mansion, Mother Selene escorted me herself, and never far or for long. I'd like to see all those things and people from my books."

"And so you shall, someday. But don't be surprised if these new experiences change your view of some things."

"What do you mean?" His shift in tone made her uneasy.

He held her at arm's length and gazed into her eyes. "The world is full of men. You might find one you like better. A warmblooded man who can walk in the sun and give you children."

"No! Don't say such things! I'll never stop loving you."

"You can't be sure of that until you've seen the outside world." Sadness shadowed his face. "Understand, my dear, if that happens, I won't keep you chained. If someone else can make you happier, I'll be glad for you."

"You won't! And I won't leave you, so stop talking about it." Tears clogged her throat and misted her eyes.

"Well, there's no need to worry about it now. Let's wait until you're actually free." He drew her head onto his chest and stroked her hair. "Meanwhile, there's a way you can sample the delights of that outside world."

"What do you mean?" She rubbed her face.

"Dream travel can lead to many possible destinations. You don't have to fly on owl wings to share it with me."

Chapter Four

ର

She woke from sleep to the awareness that, once again, she wasn't truly awake. The silvery light flooded her chamber again. Alaric's voice rang in her head: *Are you ready to travel with me?*

Yes!

Then close your eyes.

She obeyed. A rush of wind invaded the room. Her breath caught in her throat. A cyclone lifted her from the bed and swept her with dizzying speed through a dark void.

The wind's howl ceased. Her head spinning, she felt a hard surface under her feet. An arm around her waist and a hand at her elbow kept her from toppling over. She opened her eyes.

Alaric stood beside her in an anteroom with wood-paneled walls and a marble floor. Out of the silence welled the music of stringed instruments and the chatter of voices. He wore evening clothes of crimson satin and velvet, with lace at the neck and cuffs. Looking down at herself, Rapunzel discovered she wore a gown of turquoise blue with layers of petticoats under a billowing skirt. She fingered the luxurious fabric in wonder. Instead of the languid weakness after Mother Selene's spells, she felt energized. "Where are we?"

"The people of darkness gather here one night in seven," said Alaric. "This is only an ordinary soiree, of course. We hold our grand convocations at the autumnal equinox, when the nights begin to lengthen, and at midwinter, the longest night of the year."

He donned a feathered mask in the shape of an owl's head. He handed her a smaller mask, trimmed with peacock feathers, which she put on. "Shall we dance, my lady?" He offered his arm.

She rested her hand on his arm the way the magical images in her books had demonstrated. He escorted her into the ballroom. Men and women thronged the room with its vaulted ceiling and polished floor. All except the servants who circulated with trays of goblets wore fantastic masks of birds and beasts, real and mythical. She noticed their sidelong glances at her and the pride on Alaric's face as he drew her closer to his side. The music swirled around her like a gentler version of the wind that had brought her here. Dazed, she surveyed the people glittering with jewels, the candles that glowed on the sideboards, wall sconces, and chandeliers, and the long tables set with golden punchbowls.

Alaric led her to the dance set forming in the center of the room. Only then did she glance to the right of the ballroom and realize one entire wall was covered by a floor-to-ceiling mirror. She gasped and clutched Alaric's arm. In the mirror she saw herself standing alone, holding onto empty air. The vast space looked vacant except for the servants with their trays. A noise hummed in her head, as if she were about to faint.

He turned her to face away from the mirror, smoothing her hair as if comforting a nervous kitten. His eyes glowed behind the owl mask. "Don't let that frighten you. It's merely a part of what we become when we pass from ordinary life into the night world."

The buzzing in her ears faded, and she became aware of the music again. Alaric swept her into the pattern of the dance. With his hand on her waist to guide her, she glided around the floor without a misstep. She wove through the figures, transferred from Alaric to the other men in the set, each one with icy fingers and eyes that gleamed crimson behind his mask. One man in the mask of a fox smiled at her through the gap in the false jaws to show his own fangs. Lowering her eyes to hide a tremor of fear, or perhaps a quiver of arousal, she focused on the steps until another man took the place of the fox-headed one. Finally the music brought her back to her original partner.

When that dance ended, they paused at the edge of the room to watch the other guests. Rapunzel wondered how the dancers could move so gracefully in such a crowd. "I wouldn't have imagined there were this many of your kind. So many of the living dead," she said to Alaric.

"The dead far outnumber the living," he said. "Is it unbelievable that a fair number of those dead resent their status and rise to walk the earth again?"

"As spirits, maybe. After a lifetime with Mother Selene and her magic, I have no trouble believing in ghosts. But revenants with solid bodies, that's different."

"Actually, you won't often see them together in a large company like this. We're solitary creatures except for these weekly gatherings. But I did want to introduce you as my lady. My princess, to hark back to the granddams' tales."

"Does that mean my dress will turn into rags at midnight?" A laugh bubbled up at that image.

He smiled. "Our balls end at dawn, not midnight. Shall we try this new dance? They call it the waltz."

The string quartet played a different style of music now, and the dancers circled the floor as pairs instead of grouping into sets. One of Alaric's hands rested on her waist, while the other clasped her right hand. She followed his steps, at first tentatively, then floating in a smooth glide. Her heartbeat quickened, and the heat from his hand burned through the dress all the way to the quivering place at the apex of her thighs. She realized that under the layers of skirts and petticoats she wore no undergarments except gartered stockings.

Too soon the waltz ended, and Alaric guided her to the sideboard. He picked up a goblet and drank, and she did the same. A warm, salty, acrid fluid filled her mouth. Startled, she swallowed and almost gagged. Looking into the cup for the first time, she saw a thick, red liquid.

He took it from her and set it down. "Forgive me, I should have warned you not to try that one. Come over here." He led her to another punchbowl and ordered a servant to ladle a drink for her.

This time she glanced inside the goblet before sipping. This beverage was crimson, too, but thin enough to see through, and it smelled familiar. She sampled it. Ordinary red wine. By the time she finished her drink, she realized what looked odd about the serving utensils. "All the bowls and cups are gold," she said. "Real gold?"

"Yes, those who live for centuries have no trouble accumulating wealth. And we can't use silver. Its touch distresses us." He drained another goblet of hot blood and beckoned her to the dance floor again.

Hours passed in a blur. Rapunzel danced a few sets with other men and paused occasionally to converse with them and with willow-thin ladies whose laughter sounded like silver bells. She couldn't remember most of the conversations minutes after they ended.

During another waltz she found herself in the arms of the fox-masked man. He bared his fangs at her, and his eyes glowed with fierce appetite. Somehow she discovered he had steered her away from the crowd and into an alcove that led to a balcony. When he stopped dancing, the music and the guests' voices suddenly seemed distant.

She stood up straight, determined not to show fear. "What do you want, sir? I didn't mention being tired of the waltz."

"I only wanted to get a better look at Alaric's new lady." His fingers explored the nape of her neck, exposed by the elaborate knot into which her hair was coiled.

Her stomach fluttered, and a chill ran down her spine. "Very well, you've seen. Now we'd better return to the floor. I would like to rejoin Alaric now."

"What's the hurry? He's probably dancing with some other woman." The man stepped closer to her, until their bodies almost touched, and took off his fox mask. Crimson dots glowed in the centers of his dark eyes. His hawk-like profile made him look sinister as well as dashing. "Since Alaric brought you here to meet us all, I'm sure he won't mind sharing." He bent over her and licked the side of her neck.

Her chest constricted. She placed her hands on the man's shoulders and shoved, but he didn't yield. "I mind, sir! And so does he."

The man laughed and nuzzled her bare shoulder. She kicked his shin, but her soft dancing slippers had no effect. He only laughed again. Reaching under his collar, she dug her nails into his flesh. With a snarl of pain, he shook her. "Mortal bitch!"

The next instant, he was pulled off her and hurled to the ground. Alaric stood over him, growling like a wolf.

The other man got to his feet, brushed off his clothes, and retrieved his fox mask. "Enough," he snarled. "Keep her, for all I care." He stormed in the direction of the ballroom.

Rapunzel leaned against the wall, breathing hard. Alaric put his arms around her and drew her onto the balcony. "Are you all right? Did that beast wound you?"

"No." She hugged him in relief and gulped air until her pulse quieted. "He didn't even start." A cool breeze ruffled her hair, stars shone in the dark sky, and moonflower vines laden with fragrant, white blossoms draped a trellis on the balcony. "It's beautiful out here."

"Then that unpleasant encounter didn't spoil the night for you?"

"Not at all." She turned in his embrace and twined her arms around his neck. "Thank you for bringing me. I wish we never had to part." Their lips met. The taste of his mouth and the flicker of his tongue made her melt inside. She clung tighter to him, and he held her so close she had to gasp for breath. Suddenly her slit tingled and ached with hunger to sheath him. "I want to—" she murmured.

"So do I." His mouth seared her neck. He bundled up her skirts to press against her bare skin.

Through his clothes his hardness teased her. She stood on tiptoe to rub on him. "Don't you need to drink first?" she whispered.

"No, I had plenty of refreshment in there. My rod's so stiff I can't wait." His hands shook while he unbuttoned his trousers. Lifting her by the waist, he rammed into her.

Rapunzel stifled a cry and wrapped her legs around his hips. Under her clothes he thrust with frenzied haste. Her sheath rippled around him, and the explosion shuddered through her whole body.

She collapsed against him, her face damp with tears of passion.

"It's all right, my love. My beautiful one." He stroked her until her tremors ceased. When she felt normal again, they returned to the ballroom for another cup of wine and a few more dances.

Gradually Rapunzel began to notice that the chatter among the guests was becoming more subdued, sinking to faint whispers. Glancing at the tall windows opposite the mirrored wall, she realized the night sky had started to lighten toward gray. "It's almost dawn," she said to Alaric.

"Yes, we'll have to leave. I'll visit you again soon."

"What do you mean, soon?" she said, grabbing his arm. "I expect you to visit me every night."

"Not that I don't want to," he said. "But you need to rest from my demands sometimes."

"I don't want rest. I want you, always."

He drew her to the side of the room and gave her a lingering kiss. "Then I certainly wouldn't dare disappoint you."

"Every night?" she prompted.

"We'll decide that as we go along. What about your guardian, though?"

"Oh, yes, I forgot to warn you," she said. "Mother Selene visits every fortnight, at the full and new moons. You mustn't let her catch you."

"If she never varies that routine, avoiding her shouldn't be hard. I'll stay away on those nights."

"You don't have to do that. She always comes at moonrise and performs her ceremony right away. It doesn't take long. Just watch from the forest until you're sure she's left. Then you can fly up as usual."

"Very well, my princess. I only hope the change in you isn't obvious to her at first glance." With a melancholy smile, he kissed her forehead. "You have a talent for undermining my noble resolutions." He looked around. "Never mind that now. We have to go."

Rapunzel saw the walls of the ballroom turning transparent. The sky outside paled to gray. The servants collecting the empty goblets shed their flesh and became skeletons clad in tatters. The guests melted into amorphous clots of darkness, their clothes transmuting into fur or feathers. The next moment, each man or woman became a hawk, raven, fox, owl, wolf, leopard, or some other beast or bird of prey. They streamed out the open door and vanished.

The candles blew out. A whirlwind swept in through the portal and snatched up Rapunzel. A dark mist blotted out her vision.

When it cleared, she lay huddled on the floor of her bedchamber, and the sun was rising.

Chapter Five

🔊

Rapunzel's stomach knotted with worry as she waited for Mother Selene's visit on the night of the new moon. Would the sorceress notice the change in Rapunzel, as Alaric feared? On top of her nervousness about facing her guardian, she also felt impatient. For the first time, she didn't look forward to the visit as a break in her routine. Instead, Mother Selene's ritual seemed like a tedious chore she had to go through before she could welcome her lover again.

At the usual hour, Mother Selene drove her carriage to the foot of the tower, stood below the window, and called for Rapunzel to let down her hair. When she did so, the witch pronounced the arcane word, and the golden tresses grew into a network for her to climb. Rapunzel suppressed a sigh of relief. Suppose the loss of her maidenhead had somehow blocked the operation of the magic?

The witch stepped into the bedchamber and spoke the counterspell with a wave of her hand. The hair returned to normal. "Good evening, my child." Her eyes narrowed. She scanned Rapunzel up and down as if looking for changes.

Assuring herself that Mother Selene couldn't notice any difference in her, Rapunzel forced herself not to evade the witch's eyes or do anything else to reveal her nervousness. She stood motionless in her ceremonial white robe with her hands folded in front of her.

"You look tired," the witch said. "Has anything disturbed your sleep lately?"

Rapunzel's cheeks flushed. Her thoughts flashed to the latest "disturbance" in her rest, no longer ago than the previous night. How could her guardian not guess what the blush meant or hear the hammering of her pulse? "Dreams, Mother Selene," she mumbled, looking down at her feet.

"What did you say?" came the sharp demand.

"Only dreams. I've been restless with dreams the past few nights."

The witch's long fingers grasped her chin to tilt her head up. "What kind of dreams?"

"I don't remember much. Like flying." That answer was close enough to the truth that Rapunzel hoped the deception didn't show on her face.

"You look rather peaked. Thin. Are you ill?" She placed her palm on Rapunzel's cheek, then her forehead. "You don't have a fever. If anything, you feel chilled. Have you been eating properly?"

Rapunzel's skin prickled at the unwelcome touch. "I haven't been very hungry, but I'm not sick."

"You are not quite well, either. Next time I'll bring a cordial for you to drink when you retire each evening. It will restore your appetite and help you sleep peacefully."

"Thank you, Mother."

To her relief, the witch let go of her and stopped staring into her face. "I can't let you fall into poor health." Rapunzel sensed no fondness or concern in the remark, and the next sentence confirmed the impression. "If you contract some disease, it might interfere with the ritual."

She led the way up to the magic circle on the roof. As always, they took their places at opposite sides of the pentagram. The witch recited her incantations and drew the few drops of blood necessary to invoke the enchantment. The night breeze burgeoned into a supernatural wind that swirled around the two women. Rapunzel felt her hair billow like a sail in a storm and sparks dance over her body. The familiar invisible grasp tugged at her heart. Azure light erupted from the center of the pentagram and enveloped her. Across the circle, veiled in the same glow, the witch intoned the rest of the spell.

Blue lightning flashed between the two of them. The circle on the floor seethed like water in a boiling cauldron. Mother Selene whispered to it in the strange language of sorcery, but she seemed to receive no answer this time. Her voice rose in anger, and she stretched her arms toward Rapunzel.

Energy drained from Rapunzel like liquid from a cracked decanter. But she didn't see the stream of radiance that usually flowed from her to the witch. The witch's voice rose to a scream of fury that lasted for several minutes. Finally, she fell silent.

The magic stopped pressing on Rapunzel like a giant fist trying to squeeze her dry. She almost collapsed with the sudden exhaustion that turned her legs to limp rags.

With a contemptuous flip of her hand, the witch made the circle revert to darkness. "What is wrong with you?" She strode across the now-inert etching and caught Rapunzel by both arms, holding her upright. "It's clear you're useless to me for the moment. Go to your bedchamber."

Rapunzel obeyed, the older woman following her. At an impatient gesture from her guardian, she lay on the bed. Surely Mother Selene would realize the truth now, and — what? Fly into a rage and rip her to shreds?

The witch only stood over her, frowning. "You need to rest and regain your strength. Be sure to eat nourishing meals several times a day. At the full moon I shall bring the strongest healing potion I can prepare."

Rapunzel nodded, lightheaded with relief that her guardian's anger had ebbed. She had also feared that the witch would make an unscheduled visit to bring the promised cordial. Perhaps it took a long time to distill to its full strength.

"Mother Selene?" she said in a thready whisper. If she behaved even more exhausted than she felt, maybe the witch would tolerate the question she wanted to ask.

"What is it? Have you thought of some food or drink that might restore your health?"

"No, I don't need anything. I was only wondering—" She propped herself on one elbow. "I've been thinking about my future. Wondering if I'm meant to stay in this tower for the rest of my life."

The witch folded her arms and glowered. "What in the name of all the Powers put that into your head?"

"Nothing. Alone here, I have a lot of time to think."

"Why would you want to leave this refuge? You're safe here. You have everything you need. Is there anything you claim to lack?" Her voice lashed like a whip.

"No, except—well, I'm alone."

"Count your blessings, girl. Most human beings are corrupt and selfish, and many are downright dangerous. I've given you a life most young women would envy."

Rapunzel had her doubts about that claim, but she knew further argument would only provoke her guardian. "Yes, Mother."

"Could your parents who sold you have given you all these luxuries?"

"No, Mother." She closed her eyes, fighting tears.

"Then let's hear no more of this childish discontent. Concentrate on recovering so we can work together properly."

Rapunzel knew there was no "together," though. By now she realized her guardian saw her as a tool, not an acolyte or partner. She maintained a mask of submission until the witch sent up the basket of supplies and departed. With her mind in turmoil, Rapunzel lay down to wait for Alaric.

When he flew into the room and assumed his human shape, he noticed her anxiety at once. Kneeling beside the bed, he took her hand. "What's troubling you, dearest?"

"Mother Selene saw the changes in me. Sooner or later she's bound to figure out what we've done." She sat up and wiped her eyes.

He sat next to her and put his arm around her. "With her magic, that's probably true. Your blood must have altered by now."

She snuggled close to him, laying her head on his shoulder. "What can I possibly do about her suspicions?"

"I could stop feeding on you for a while, to make your blood run pure again. Or I could leave you alone altogether."

"No, I couldn't bear that!" Pressing her fingers to his temples, Rapunzel turned his head and raised her mouth to his. The nibble of his lips and the flicker of his tongue made her tremble with longing. Desire coiled in her loins, and she thought she could sense the hunger gnawing at the pit of his stomach.

He pulled away, leaving her panting for air. He heaved a shuddering sigh before he spoke. "That might not solve the problem in any case. If the arcane value of your blood depends on your virginity, it's too late already." He rubbed her back until her breathing settled to normal. "We have to discuss this rationally. I don't want to give you up. I would wither like a dry tree. But I can't let my needs condemn you to the witch's wrath."

"Don't forget I need you, too. There must be some way we can stay together."

"The obvious solution is for you to leave this tower," he said. "If you want to."

"I certainly don't want to spend my life here, which seems to be Mother Selene's plan. Especially after those dream travels with you. I want to learn about the outside world firsthand. I have books to teach me, but they're not enough anymore."

"Yes, I remember you mentioned those books," he said. "Why don't you show them to me?"

Though she suspected the request was mainly intended as a distraction from her unhappiness, she agreed. Hand in hand, they walked downstairs to the sitting room on the second level. From the bookcase she chose a guide to courtly etiquette. They sat on the divan under the latticed window and turned the pages together. "I never expect to need these lessons," said Rapunzel. "But I used to enjoy reading them and imagining myself at a state dinner or a noblewoman's soiree." She showed Alaric a passage about how to set a banquet table and which fork or spoon to use for each course. On the pages, miniature people in powdered wigs and velvet gowns or satin waistcoats sampled food from silver plates and bowls.

"Very entertaining magic," he said, caressing the back of her neck. "I hope someday you'll be able to attend a banquet like this."

"That might be interesting," she said, "except I don't think I'd care for one of those silly wigs."

Laughing, he flipped the pages to a scene of a formal dance. The printed figures circled in stately patterns on the shiny ballroom floor.

"Like the masquerade I dreamed about that other night. I remembered this lesson, and it helped me keep up with the steps." She frowned. "Was that real or not? I felt as if I was really there."

He clasped her hand. "It was a vision we shared in sleep, but on some plane of existence it actually happened."

Rapunzel shook her head. "I don't understand."

"Nor do I. As I told you, I gained this power with my transformation. I don't comprehend its working." His thumb circled the palm of her hand.

Shivering, she closed the book. "I don't want to talk about things I may never be able to enjoy. Let's not waste the time we could be enjoying another way." She guided his hand to her breast.

He gently removed it, barely skimming her nipple through the cloth. "Dearest, I shouldn't feast on you every night. Your health will suffer."

"Why should I care about that?" The bitter tinge in her voice surprised even her. "If I'm doomed to spend the rest of my life here, it might as well be a short one."

"That won't happen if I can help it." Cupping the back of her head, he lightly kissed her.

When he started to withdraw, she twined her arms around his neck and fastened her mouth to his. She extended her tongue to probe his lips until they parted. With an inarticulate murmur, he yielded, and his tongue teased hers.

The now-familiar warmth suffused her body. He placed a hand on her knee and stroked her through the silk of her nightgown. The fabric sliding over her skin made her squirm with impatience for a more intimate touch. Slowly he worked his way up her thigh. Breaking off the kiss, she rose onto her knees, arched her back, and rubbed her cheek and the side of her neck against his lips.

He shook his head. "No, I mustn't risk draining more than you can spare. I can satisfy you without feeding on you." His tongue flicked along her jawline back to her mouth.

Meanwhile, his hand reached her mound and caressed her through the cloth.

How could his touch burn when his flesh felt so cool the rest of the time? Heat ignited in her breasts and between her legs. Her sheath ached to be filled. She felt dizzy with longing.

His fingers slipped between the folds of her slit, rubbing through the silk, which soon became soaked with her wetness. "Your sweet dew," he whispered against her mouth. "I want to taste it."

That image made her head spin and her pulse race. His fingertips found her bud and circled the tip until it throbbed in release.

Almost fainting, she threw her head back and reclined on the divan. Alaric knelt on the carpet and flipped up the skirt of her gown. "Your scent — delicious —" He nibbled his way up the inside of one thigh, never piercing the skin. She arched her hips, silently begging for him to reach the place that ached and twitched with need.

His tongue dipped into her slit. Her inner muscles clenched at the bolt of sensation that shot through her. The next moment, his fingers replaced his tongue, and he licked her bud. It swelled to unbearable tightness. Clutching the divan and digging her nails into the cushions, she thrust toward him. One of his arms wrapped around her waist to keep his mouth in position while she bucked in uncontrollable frenzy. His tongue flicked until her whole body convulsed with the pulsing of her most tender parts, and her sheath contracted around his fingers.

"Now," she gasped, "drink. You need it."

"I don't," he said, his cheek resting on her stomach. "I feasted on your honey."

"You still need more. My blood. You can't lie to me." She reached down and used a fingernail to scrape a bleeding line on her inner thigh. Her breath hitched at the momentary pain.

"Rapunzel, you shouldn't have." He nuzzled the scratch.

"If you had used your teeth, it wouldn't have hurt."

With a growl of surrender, he licked the wound in long, slow laps. She gasped at the touch of his hot, wet tongue so near her sensitized flesh. Answering that silent appeal, he caressed her with his fingers while he sampled her blood. She needed only a few strokes to make her soar to another peak.

At last he stood up and rearranged her gown. "Now I'd better leave before you tempt me again. Enchantress."

She responded to his teasing grin with a weak smile. She felt drained, just as he'd cautioned, but in a thoroughly pleasurable way. Instead of trying to entice him into another embrace, she accepted his farewell, escorted him upstairs, and watched him fly into the distance. Lying down, she fell asleep instantly but had no dream adventures.

Chapter Six

ω

He visited her every evening for the next fortnight. She developed the habit of sleeping most of each day, to be wide awake for his embraces. Though her vitality began to ebb, she hardly noticed, because the moment he touched her, she caught fire.

On the eve of the full moon, as they said their farewell, he seemed more somber than usual. At the window he enfolded her in his arms. "Come away with me tomorrow night."

"How? The tower has no door, and you say you don't have that kind of magic."

He laughed softly. "We'll manage. I'll bring a rope ladder. The challenge will be to escape without the witch stopping us."

Rapunzel clung to him and rubbed her cheek against his chest. "Why can't I just explain to Mother Selene what we've done and ask her to release me? If my blood doesn't work in her rituals anymore, why would she try to keep me from finding happiness somewhere else?"

"My dear, do you still believe she cares for you? She'll be enraged when she discovers you've lost your maidenhead."

"What could be so important about my blood, anyway?"

"I believe it serves as payment to the forces that maintain her in the prime of life. You say she hasn't changed in all the years you've known her. Who knows how old she actually is?"

Rapunzel shivered at the memory of Mother Selene's icy eyes. The few times the witch's wrath had broken upon her like a thunderstorm, its fury had terrified her. She had no desire to face that storm again. "All right, I'll go with you. Can't we leave tomorrow before sunset, so I won't have to deal with her at all?"

"Unfortunately, I can't fly up to you until after dark. Sunlight weakens me and keeps me from changing form. We'll have to wait for her to make her visit and depart, just to be safe, and then hope she'll have no way to sense your escape. That way, we should have two weeks before she realizes you've disappeared."

"Won't we have a long journey to get out of her reach? The forest stretches from the tower all the way to the mountains."

Again his chest vibrated with laughter. "That's a magical illusion. In fact, there are towns within an hour's ride. I have a home in one of them, a house with a garden of night-blooming flowers. With doors and gates that open freely." His cool lips brushed her forehead. "I'll come for you after the witch's visit. Until tomorrow night, my love."

* * * * *

On the night of the full moon, Rapunzel waited for the witch with a dry throat and racing heart. The usual call came: "Rapunzel, Rapunzel, let down your hair."

When Mother Selene climbed into the chamber, her narrow-eyed stare made it clear that she'd instantly noticed a change. "Child, you look pale. You are ill after all, aren't you?"

Hastily, Rapunzel stammered, "Not ill, Mother. But I do have something to tell you. To ask you." Nervously she rubbed her throat.

The witch gripped her chin and tilted her head up in the lamplight. "What's that on your neck?" She ran her fingers over the scratch and bent closer to peer at it.

"Dark Powers! It can't be!" Her pale face flushed with anger. "Who has violated you?" Before Rapunzel could gather her wits to pull away, the witch whipped out her silver dagger and pierced Rapunzel's wrist. She caught a droplet of blood on her fingertip and tasted it. "It is! Your blood is tainted! No wonder the spell went bad last time."

"Please, Mother Selene, listen to me!"

"Shut your mouth, you ungrateful slut!" She slammed her fist hard into the side of Rapunzel's head.

Rapunzel heard a crack, felt a lightning bolt of pain, and fell. Her head struck the corner of the bedside table. Just as she hit the floor, darkness swallowed her.

* * * * *

She woke in her own bed. Her head pounded, and her neck felt sore. The oil lamp no longer burned, but somehow she could see better than the moonlight should have allowed. Mother Selene crouched at one side of the window, below the level of the sill. She held the silver athame in her right hand.

Rapunzel's body felt encased in ice. She welcomed her frozen condition, for she didn't want the witch to notice she was conscious. She couldn't tell how many minutes passed before she heard Alaric's voice at the foot of the tower, "Rapunzel, where are you? May I come in?"

No, Alaric, go away, danger! If only she could whisper the warning directly into his mind. She dared not cry out. Why did he approach the tower with Mother Selene's horse and carriage in plain sight? Maybe the witch had rendered them invisible. When Rapunzel didn't answer, surely Alaric would realize something was wrong.

Then she heard a soft reply. "Yes, my love, come up." The witch's imitation sounded exactly like Rapunzel's voice, as far as the girl could tell.

Tears trickled from her half-closed eyes. Why couldn't Alaric sense the trap? In despair, she cast aside all thought of her own safety. Let the witch kill her. What would her life matter if her lover died? She struggled to force a scream from her throat. Paralysis held her silent.

The flapping of wings reached her ears, and the bird's silhouette appeared at the window. He swooped inside and changed to his human form. He looked around, puzzled. "Rapunzel?"

The witch leapt to her feet, brandishing the dagger. "You ruined her for me. Your little pet is dead, and so are you." With a roar of magically-charged fury, she plunged the silver blade into Alaric's chest. He howled in pain. The witch thrust the knife to the hilt into his heart, planted both hands on his shoulders, and shoved him out the window.

Her lover's death scream shattered Rapunzel's immobility. She sprang from the bed and knocked the witch to the floor. A wave of power swept over Rapunzel. She pinned the woman's arms and heard herself snarling like a wolf.

When Mother Selene tried and failed to shake off the girl's grip, the anger in her eyes changed to fear. "You're dead!" she shrieked. "I killed you!"

Rapunzel's lips involuntarily curled back from her teeth. A burning in her throat and stomach blotted out thought. Her hands shifted from the witch's arms to the skull and, in one swift twist, snapped the spine. She plunged her teeth into the woman's neck.

Blood gushed into her mouth, as intoxicating as hot, spiced wine. She gulped it down until the thirst abated and the witch's body started to grow cool.

Rapunzel stood up with a shudder of revulsion and staggered to the washbasin on the table, where she cleaned the woman's blood from her hands and face. The room looked different. A faint, fading glow surrounded the body on the floor. Her eyes saw all other objects in soft pastels instead of the blacks and grays of night. To her astonishment, the tapestries and bed linens turned to rags before her eyes. Paint on walls and window frames grayed and peeled. An odor of mildew tainted the air. When she glanced at the corpse, she found the hair grizzled, the hands withered into claws, and the woman's face a spiderweb of wrinkles over the contours of the skull.

Hurrying to the window, she stared down at the clearing and saw Alaric lying on his back in the grass. Near the edge of the forest, the horse grazed placidly in its harness. If Mother Selene had cast a spell of invisibility, her death had broken that spell. In the distance, lights of scattered villages glowed, lights Rapunzel had never seen before.

Am I trapped here now? she wondered. Tears scalded her cheeks as she gazed at Alaric's body, the dagger hilt protruding from his chest. She stretched her arms out, yearning for him. A surge of power crackled through her. She felt her legs draw up, her arms shrink, feathers sprout from her skin. She launched herself into the air. In the form of a huge owl, she soared out the window and spiraled to the ground.

Hardly aware of how she achieved the change, she willed herself back into woman-shape and fell to her knees beside Alaric. With her new strength, she yanked the knife out of his heart and threw it aside.

Sobbing, she tore open his shirt and kissed the stab wound. The elixir of his blood seared her lips. "Wake up, please, you can't die!" She slashed her wrist with her teeth and squeezed blood into the gash in his chest.

The edges of the wound grew together before her eyes. He emitted a low moan. Rapunzel flung her arms around him, nestled into his shoulder, and heard the laborious thud of his heart. Glancing up, she saw his eyelids flutter.

"Rapunzel?" he whispered. "My love?"

"You're alive!" She could hardly breathe for astonishment. Her heart pounded against her ribs.

"Almost. I need…"

She wiggled on top of him until his mouth nuzzled the curve of her neck. His fangs pierced her skin and shot the now familiar lightning bolt through her. The tightness of her nipples and the gush of heat between her legs made her squirm with eagerness. She felt his blood-engorged erection stiffen and press against the V of her secret place.

She sat up, straddling his hips, hoisted the skirt of her gown, and unfastened his trousers. The moment she ripped them open, his rod sprang free. She impaled herself on it. Her growls of pleasure mingled with his as he plunged into her wet grotto. With an urgent groan, he wrapped his arms around her to pull her down to his hungry lips.

Her transformed blood spurted into his mouth at the same moment his seed fountained into her. She clung to him, trembling in ecstasy at the completion of their love circle.

Long minutes passed before their passion exhausted itself. She burrowed into his arms with a sigh of satisfaction.

"You've joined me, just as we agreed, though I didn't mean to rob you of your choice this way. I never imagined the witch would slay you and force the change." He sat up and helped her to her feet. "Do you regret becoming a creature of the night?"

Stretching her arms wide to invite the cool breeze, she inhaled the tangy scents of the forest and its animal life. "Of course not. It means freedom."

Margaret L. Carter

A crackling noise reached her ears. The tower shuddered, stones crumbling away from it. "The witch's enchantments are dissolving," he said. "We must leave, now!" With an arm around her waist, he turned her toward the edge of the clearing where the horse and carriage waited. Behind the carriage, a broad path she had never seen before led into the trees. "Will you come with me to my home," asked Alaric, "and be my princess?"

"With the greatest joy, my lord of the night." She entwined arms with him and walked toward her new life.

Dragon's Tribute

ഉ

Chapter One

By the time sunset reddened the horizon, the procession of village elders had vanished. Rowena squinted through her tears to watch the last of them retreat into the woods along the path winding back to town. Back to their safe homes and barred doors. No one wanted to risk meeting the dragon. Not the elders, the parish priest and curate, or the Baron's chaplain. Not his men at arms, who had stood guard to keep the peace during the offering of tribute. Not even his dark-robed household wizard. Not her neighbors, who had acted friendly enough until this day came. Least of all Rowena herself, chosen for the creature's annual feast. With the fading daylight, the poppy-tinctured wine began to wear off. Fear trickled through her veins. Her throat, still raw from the crying she'd done before the priests had dosed her, was parched with thirst.

Already numbness crept up her bound arms. She strained against the rope that tied her to the withered tree at the verge of the stony foothills where no shepherds dared graze their flocks. The edge of the dragon's land. She choked down the scream that welled in her throat. Nobody would come to her rescue. Anyway, if released, where could she go? Any of the hamlets that owed allegiance to the local Baron would cast her out if she begged for refuge. It was considered a dire omen for a dragon's sacrifice to return alive. Rowena's own grandmother had been driven from her home in a distant land for that very reason.

Rowena tried to find comfort in her grandmother's amulet hanging from a thong around her neck, hidden under the traditional white shift. Grandmother had slipped the charm over Rowena's head at the last moment. According to Grandmother, the bronze disk had enabled her to escape alive from a dragon's lair. Her native village had exiled her for fear that the dragon's rejection would bring a curse upon the community. After months of wandering she had found her way here and given birth to Rowena's mother

A breeze sprang up, drying the clammy sweat on Rowena's bare limbs. A chill prickled on her skin, despite the season. Every Midsummer Eve the dragon swooped down at sunset to collect his annual tribute. As tradition demanded, the Baron and the priests had cast lots to determine which town would supply the maiden. The lot had fallen upon Rowena's village, and within the village, her name had been chosen. Of course the lot never fell upon the Baron's household, a village elder's daughter, or a priest's sister. This year, with sickness rampant among the local children, the choice had not been left to chance. Rowena knew she had been sacrificed because of her grandmother's dubious past, suspected of having unleashed a curse upon the community.

Rowena squirmed to work her way around the tree until she faced the hillside instead of the path to the village. The rope scraped her wrists. She saw no bones scattered nearby. Maybe the monster carried his victims to his lair instead of devouring them on the spot. She prayed that if the amulet didn't protect her, the end would come quickly. Would his jaws bite her head off, or would he first incinerate her in a roar of flame? On countless winter nights she had listened avidly to the ballads and tales Grandmother had picked up while wandering the countryside and wished she could live those adventures. Now she would have emitted a bitter laugh at her silly notions of adventure, if her throat hadn't been clogged with fear.

A winged shape glided toward her from the peaks in the distance. Her chest tightened, and her heart hammered against her ribs.

The creature loomed before her like a giant bat as it sank to the ground. Her unbound hair blew in the wind it stirred up. It settled in front of her and folded the wings on its back.

Her stomach cramped with terror, although the dragon looked smaller than she'd expected. She had imagined him as large as a church or perhaps even so huge his wings would blot out the sun. Still, at twice the size of the Baron's warhorse, the monster was fearsome enough. Instead of thick-bodied like a horse, though, he looked sinuously elongated, with a serpentine tail.

His crested head, with jaws the length of her forearm, lowered toward her. Holding her breath, she waited for the dagger-size teeth to rend her throat. Her legs trembled. The glittering eyes fixed upon her. She squeezed her own eyes shut. His hot breath blasted her in the face. It smelled like a bonfire of pine branches with a trace of incense.

Something like a scorching whip lashed her neck. She choked back a scream. Now the fangs would pierce her flesh.

But they didn't. Hissing, the dragon withdrew his tongue, the "whip" she'd felt. When she dared to look, he was staring at her with his oval, slanted eyes—the color of emeralds. Not that she had ever seen an emerald up close, but she could think of no other word for that green glow.

He stretched one of his front feet toward her. His claws touched the skin just above the neckline of her shift. She couldn't suppress a whimper. The dragon withdrew his talons and used them to snap the ropes that bound her to the tree trunk. Her legs crumpled. The dragon's leg wrapped around her like a cat's paw scooping up a mouse.

With a cry, Rowena shoved against the scaly chest. It felt smoother than she'd imagined and as warm as the outside of an oven. A rainbow of greens, blues, and violets rippled over the creature's hide, as if coated with powdered gems. No wonder legends claimed kings would pay a fortune for a dragon's skin.

There was no knight here to slay this beast, though, and no matter how beautiful, he would still devour her. Tears trickled down Rowena's cheeks.

The next moment, panic dried them. The dragon leaped into the air and spread his wings. Her stomach lurched. She swallowed bile. A scream ripped from her throat. The dragon spun her around to face away from him and clutched her against his chest with both forefeet. Wind whipped her hair and stung her eyes. Her legs dangling, she gripped the creature's front limbs and babbled a frantic prayer. Better to get her throat slashed by his fangs than fall to the rocky ground and perhaps writhe in agony for hours with a broken spine.

With her back to the dragon's body, she could see the rocky hills ahead. In the dying light she saw they were heading for a dark gash in a cliff above a ravine. After several minutes of flight, the dragon glided to a stop on a ledge barely wide enough to hold him. No wonder the Baron's men at arms had never stormed the dragon's lair. Only something with wings could reach this entrance.

The dragon put her down and nudged her inside. She stumbled, fell to her knees, and crouched there, shaking. The nausea subsided to mild queasiness. She looked up at the dragon, who towered on his rear legs in the "doorway." His wings, though shaped like a bat's, weren't black or brown, but iridescent with shades of emerald and turquoise.

She almost fainted when he spoke to her: "Get up, girl." She had to think a second to understand the guttural phrase. She couldn't tell how he formed the words, with his mouth open but not moving. His voice rumbled and made the nerves quiver in the pit of her stomach.

When she didn't move, he hooked his claws around her elbow and dragged her upright. The floor of the cave felt like polished marble under her bare feet, instead of the rough stone she expected. A pearly glow emanated from the walls, weaker than the sun, but she could see much clearer than in moonlight.

"Walk," the dragon growled. His tongue snaked out to lash her arm. Shivering, she obeyed. He slithered into the cavern after her.

The entry tunnel opened into a huge chamber with a vaulted ceiling, much higher than the roof of the village church or the Baron's hall. Through a rift far overhead she glimpsed the gray of the evening sky, rapidly dying toward night. Several portals opened off this central room. At the far end lay a heap of gems and coins. So the tales about the dragon's treasure hoard were true. If she could escape from this lair and take a handful of those jewels along, she could flee to some far country as a rich woman.

She reminded herself that she couldn't escape, not unless she learned how to fly or to crawl down the cliff like an insect. Besides, no doubt the dragon would kill and feast on her this very night.

He prodded her toward an alcove near the pile of treasure. Satin cushions filled the space, with covers of silk and finely woven wool spread over them. The dragon pushed Rowena, and she collapsed onto her back. His talons snagged the upper edge of her shift. He tore it down the front, leaving her naked body exposed.

Her skin prickled. Now he would surely rip her heart out.

He sniffed her, and his muzzle touched the amulet. One claw plucked at the disk, about the size of a woman's palm, etched with a dragon's profile and encircled by runic symbols. Raising his head, he snorted a puff of smoke. "S-s-s-so...what is thisss?" He nudged her again.

The long, sinuous tongue circled her neck and snaked between her breasts. Bolts of heat and cold shot through her.

Knowing the dragon understood human language gave her the courage to speak. "Are you going to kill me now?" She gripped the amulet. It hadn't kept the beast from carrying her off, but at least she wasn't dead yet.

He raised his formidable head. "Kill? Why?" His breath behind the words hissed like a snake's. The sound echoed in the vast chamber.

"To eat me."

"I did not bring you here as food." Now that her ears became attuned to his speech, she understood him more easily.

"Then what—" Her voice came out as a thin squeak. "Didn't you devour the other girls?"

A puff of smoke displayed his contempt for that question. "I burned to ash the ones who died of sickness or starved themselves to death. Those who lived longer, I set free at the turn of autumn."

Was he lying? Dragons had a reputation for deviousness. "None of them came home, that I ever heard." Possibly because they feared the kind of reception her grandmother had suffered?

"I am not to blame for that." He loomed over her, and again she felt and smelled his hot, incense-scented breath.

With his clawed forefeet he tugged off the remnants of the shift. Again his tongue tasted the hollow of her throat and swept down the front of her body. It circled each breast in turn. She shuddered with each lash of the whip-like appendage. If he didn't want her as food, why did he seem to be testing her flavor?

She forced herself to lie still, her nails digging into the fabric under her. The dragon's tongue spiraled around one breast, tightening the circle until the forked tip brushed the nipple. Rowena let out a yelp of surprise. Swallowing, she stared into the emerald eyes and prayed the noise wouldn't provoke him into biting her. Instead of sinking his fangs into her flesh, he licked the nipple. It hardened the way it did in cold air on winter mornings. The other nipple crinkled up at the same time. Shivers not completely unpleasant prickled her bare skin.

The rapid flutter of the dragon's tongue made her tremble with renewed waves of fire and ice. She wondered how she could feel chills when his breath almost scorched. The untouched nipple tingled in sympathy with the one he was tormenting. Hardly aware of her own action, she moved one hand to her breast, cupped it, and flicked the nipple with her thumb. That touch brought some relief, but an ache grew in both breasts and spread over her body to the pit of her stomach. Wetness collected between her legs.

The dragon licked his way from one nipple to the other, displacing her hand. His tongue danced over her breasts, teasing each one in turn. Her hand, meanwhile, slid downward to cover the hair on her mound. Tracing circles on her chest and belly, the dragon's tongue seared her with painless heat. She imagined if she looked at her skin, she would see forked patterns etched there.

While he lapped her stomach and thighs, she rubbed her nipples. She would have cringed in shame if any man had seen her easing her own aches that way, but a winged, fanged monster didn't matter. The tongue flicked faster, up and down her inner thighs. The clawed forefeet pushed her hands aside and rested on her breasts. On each side, a curved claw scraped the nipple lightly, drawing no blood, but making each taut peak tickle unbearably.

His tongue-tip brushed the nubbin nested in the damp folds between her legs. She gasped and flinched.

"Delicious," the dragon hissed. He sampled the wetness gathering in her slit.

Now he would surely tear her to shreds. Her stomach knotted, and her heart raced with mingled terror and excitement. In the midst of her fear, her flesh still throbbed from the relentless licking. A hot flush spread over her whole body.

The length of his tongue slid between her thighs and snaked up her slit to the swollen bud. She moaned and clenched her fists in the bunched-up silk she lay on. The dragon licked up her moist cleft, down, and up again over and over. Her bud twitched with impatience whenever the tongue-tip stopped licking it.

Rowena wasn't completely untouched in her private parts. She'd fondled herself many times in her bed in the loft on summer nights, holding her breath for fear of waking her parents. And she had spent hours in secret frolic with Will, the baker's son, with his fingers probing her slit and tickling the nubbin at the top, while she rubbed his cock through his breeches. Because his father would never allow him to marry a poor farm girl of dubious ancestry, they hadn't risked a bedding that might get her with child. Still, she knew the feel of carnal pleasure.

But Will's fumbling had never caused such exquisite torment as this. She trembled all over. Now the dragon's claws clutched her thighs to hold them apart. The sharp points stung but didn't gouge deeply enough to produce real pain. The tongue whipped faster and faster. Her bud quivered. Her inner muscles rippled. She needed to squeeze her legs together, but the dragon wouldn't let go of them. She arched her back, screaming.

His tongue flickered over her bud while convulsions of release ripped through her.

When the tremors stopped, she lay flat on her back, gasping for air.

The dragon licked the scrapes his claws left on her inner thighs. "Deliciousss," he hissed again. His tail curved around to lie across her legs.

She placed a timid hand on the side of his neck. The warm smoothness of the iridescent scales fascinated her. Under his glittering, emerald eyes, she felt like a bird in a snake's coils.

He exhaled a puff of smoke. It startled her anew when he rumbled deep in his chest, "Are you sated?"

"What?" She flinched and emitted a stifled cry when he gave one of her nipples a casual lick.

"You still show signs of fear. I would not have you cower from me. Perhaps you need more pleasuring."

"More — ?"

"To make you fully open for me. Here, perhaps." He snuffled her neck and lightly licked it. Shivers raced over her bare skin. "Or here." His breath heated the hollow between her breasts.

Her nipples crinkled when his tongue grazed them. The flutter in her stomach started again. Her legs trembled. While he lapped his way down her body, his tail slithered over her thighs and insinuated its tip between them. Without thinking, she parted her legs. The tail-point probed her slit.

She jerked in surprise and let out an involuntary yelp.

"Have you never been penetrated?" the rumbling voice asked.

A blush suffused her body. "I'm a maiden. The sacrifice has to be a virgin."

With a curlicue of smoke from his nostrils, the dragon said, "Indeed? I never gave any such command. Your kind have strange notions."

Of course, Rowena mused, why should the monster care about the state of his dinner's maidenhead? The thought pierced her with renewed fear. A fear that flew out of her mind when the end of his tail began stroking up and down the cleft between her moist folds. A gush of wetness welled up. She clasped her thighs to trap the appendage between them.

The pressure on her slit and the button nestled in the damp hair erased all terror and shame. She found herself rocking her hips in time to the dragon's rapid licking of her nipples and belly. He chased the unbearable tingling from one point to the next so fast her head whirled. The tail-tip tickled her button until it throbbed, and her sheath pulsed until she almost fainted in the exquisite delirium.

At last his tail, tongue, and claws withdrew. Rowena opened her eyes.

Panting, her skin dampened with sweat, she gazed up at the dragon. He reared on his back legs, exposing his belly.

He roared a gout of flame toward the ceiling. His penis stood up, thicker and longer than a stallion's, inflamed to a lurid scarlet.

She scrabbled backward, eyes widening in alarm. The thought of getting ravished by that weapon terrified her more than a quick death from his fangs.

While she stared, though, the organ receded out of sight like a horse's. He grasped her arms and pulled her to her feet. "Come along, you need food and refreshment."

Dazed, she didn't resist while he guided her to one of the side chambers, just big enough to hold his serpentine length. There she found a pool with a miniature waterfall flowing into one end. The other end of the pool bubbled with steam and a faint egg-like aroma. A linen sheet lay folded on the floor. On a shelf in the stone wall sat a silver pitcher and goblet and a bowl filled with peaches and berries.

"Be quick," the dragon growled.

When he disappeared into the main room, she let out a long, shuddering sigh. The knot in her chest loosened for the first time since her neighbors had dragged her to the tree of sacrifice. Checking the pitcher, she discovered it held pale, crisp wine. She poured a glass and drank, then found her stomach cramping with hunger despite her fear. She dubiously examined the bowl of fruit, which she had always heard caused sickness if eaten raw. With no other food in sight, though, she decided to take a chance. She gobbled a peach, its sticky juice trickling down her chin. A circuit of the chamber revealed a niche containing a chamber pot. If the dragon provided all these necessities, could he be telling the truth about keeping her instead of slaughtering her? Or did the caresses and wine only serve to lull her and the food to fatten her for a later meal?

And another fear invaded her thoughts. The priest's homilies called Satan "the old dragon." Could this monster be a demon in reptile shape, damning her to Hell by seducing her into wantonness?

To her shame, she realized she would rather submit to his seduction than have her bones scattered in the ravine below the cave. If letting him goad her to heights of ecstasy would prolong her life, she would gladly embrace that fate. She could always repent later.

Remembering her captor's instruction to hurry, she stepped into the hot end of the spring. She didn't want the creature to interrupt before she could have a bath. The water, just hot enough to bear, made her skin tingle. Bubbles clustered around her. She immersed herself up to her neck, gulped a deep breath, and plunged her head in to soak her hair. The sensation felt nothing like her weekly hip-bath at home or even the occasional dip in the weed-clogged stream that served the village mill. She stood up and waded toward the cold end of the pool, delighted by the gradual change in temperature from hot through warm to chilly.

A low growl from the entrance snapped her back to reality. How could she enjoy anything while imprisoned in a monster's lair? She scrambled out of the water and dried herself with the linen cloth, wrapping the least damp section of it around her like a gown. The cool air of the cave made her nipples tighten. Her legs trembling, she tiptoed into the central chamber.

The dragon hooked a claw-tip in the fabric that draped her body. "Remove this. I will give you clothing—later." He waved his other forefoot at the treasure heap, where she noticed a couple of large chests she'd overlooked before.

Melting inside at the heat of his breath, she unwrapped the linen and let it fall. In the chill of the den, shivers crept over her.

With his emerald eyes glowing, the creature's gaze raked up and down her. "Perhaps you are the one I have waited for. What is your name?"

"Rowena," she whispered.

He snorted small puffs of smoke from his nostrils. "Human names are so short and crude."

She raised her chin and wrapped her arms around her breasts. "What's yours, then?"

"Too complex for you. Call me Viridiseffulgentissimus."

Even that was beyond her grasp, a meaningless tangle of noise. "How about Virid?"

"If you must," he rumbled. His talons stretched to touch her. The point of one claw pierced the curve of her breast just below the amulet, drawing a bead of blood.

She flinched. Now at last he would rip her apart and devour her.

His tongue licked the spot. But instead of crushing her spine between his jaws, he backed up, reared onto his hind legs, and shimmered. "Yesss. As I sussspected."

Rowena stared at him, stunned, clutching the bronze disk dangling from her neck. His outline blurred and dissolved. The enormous reptilian body shrank, enveloped in a cloud of green fog. When the mist evaporated, a dragon no longer towered over her.

A tall, naked man with olive skin and emerald eyes stood there instead. His silver-blue hair grew in a crest like the one on the dragon's head. When he moved closer, Rowena noticed his skin had tiny scales like those of a fish. Hesitantly touching his arm, though, she discovered he felt dry and warm, just as he had in dragon shape.

"You—changed." She could hardly breathe. Her head spun with confusion. "How? Magic?" She had never seen a nude man before. In her dalliance with young Will, she had played with his cock, but it hadn't felt anywhere near the size of the dragon-man's organ.

"All dragons have this magic." His voice sounded deep and resonant, with a hint of the beast's growl. "From that sample of your blood, I knew the moment was right." He wrapped his arms around her. Her nipples peaked at the contact with his chest. He grew hard against her lower abdomen.

Her head reeled in bewilderment. "The moment—? What do you mean?"

"Later. Do not trouble yourself now." He stroked her back, making her spine arch like a cat's. "Beautiful," he whispered.

She glanced at her arms, sun-browned in contrast to the whiteness of the parts usually covered by clothes. "Me? Oh, no." A half-hysterical giggle bubbled in her throat.

Twining a lock of her hair around his fingers, he said, "You should have a name that speaks of your golden tresses and your delectable sweetness." Instead of a hiss, his voice now carried a hint of a purr.

She felt herself blushing. None of the village lads had ever said anything of this kind. "No, a crude human name is good enough for me."

He laughed, a sound like a silver bell. "Rowena, were you content in your other life?"

Other life? As if she had a prospect of a new one? She shook her head, in confusion rather than denial. "I knew nothing different."

"What was it like?"

She rubbed her eyes, trying to collect her thoughts. "I scrubbed laundry and cooked and cleaned with Mamma, tended my little brothers, helped in the vegetable garden, milked the goats. People thought we were a bit strange because of Grandmother, so I didn't have any close friends. But I guess I was happy." She'd never questioned the matter before. Now she realized she scarcely knew what "happy" meant.

He stroked her hair. "What about your grandmother?"

"She came from a distant village as a young woman, pregnant with my mother. She said she'd escaped from a dragon. Like you."

"Indeed?" His hand ran down her back to cup her arse. She let out an involuntary moan and pressed tighter against him.

"She gave me this charm to protect me, but I guess it didn't work, because you took me anyway. People thought she was cursed because that other dragon threw her out or let her go. Some of the other girls used to say we were lucky the village elders let us live there at all. When typhoid fever began to rage among the children this past month, people accused our family of causing it, because we carried a curse from Grandmother. The elders thought sacrificing me would make it stop." Tears welled in her eyes.

"You can forget about them," he said. His palm caressed her back in slow swirls. His breath ruffled her hair. "You will never go back. You belong to me now." He picked her up and carried her to the sleeping alcove. "I gave you pleasure, did I not? Now I will take my satisfaction."

Her stomach knotted with apprehension. This creature — Virid — was no longer a winged monster, but a ravishing young man, however strange in appearance. Swiving with him would count as fornication.

She reminded herself that she had no other choice except a gruesome death. Surely preserving her life was the right thing to do.

The satin-draped pillows felt cool under Rowena's back. Virid reclined on his side next to her. He played with her long hair, using a lock of it to tease her breast. "Are you still afraid?"

The tickle on her naked flesh made her squirm. "Why shouldn't I be?"

His eyebrows arched. "I have told you I mean no harm. Let me show you." He edged closer and licked behind her ear. His teeth caught the earlobe, and a jolt of excitement shot through her. His hard cock pressed against her flank. "You do understand what I want of you?"

"Of course! I'm no child. I've watched the billy goats mating with the nannies." Her cheeks grew hot. "You want to put your—member inside me."

"Yes, but only when you are fully prepared." Nibbling her ear again, he nipped his way along her jaw to her mouth.

Her lips involuntarily parted. When he tasted the corners of her mouth, her own tongue darted to meet his. The spark ignited a fire in the pit of her stomach. Her nipples and the muscles inside her tightened.

His hand skimmed over her body and covered the triangle of hair. She writhed on the cushions while he kissed her mouth and probed between her nether lips. Breaking off the kiss to lick a path to her breast, he murmured, "Your pearl glistens with dew." His thumb circled the "pearl" to emphasize the point. Gasping, she arched her back.

He laughed softly, making her skin prickle. "Tell me what you want."

"Rub it! Please—"

He strummed the spot while his two long middle fingers entered her canal. Her button felt tight enough to burst. When it began to throb and her sheath pulsed in the same rhythm, Virid thrust his fingers deep inside. A twinge of pain shocked her into a yelp of protest.

He pulled out and stroked her gently until she stopped shuddering. "Forgive me. That was part of the preparation." He parted her legs and bent to nuzzle the patch of hair between them. "Your flesh is like a ripe fruit." He licked the gap between the folds. "Like a pomegranate with a single seed."

The "seed" tingled at the flick of his tongue. Coated with a sheen of sweat, limp from the aftershocks of her release,

Rowena didn't feel the previous burning inside, only languid pleasure.

"So soft, like silk," he murmured, humming against her tender parts. Waves of warmth rippled through her. He moved up to lie above her and rub his rigid shaft on her mound. "I need you now," he said in a voice rough with urgency.

The friction made her melt all over again. "Yes. Now."

"Do not fear, this will go quickly." His breath came faster. "It has been a very long time since I last mated. Over a hundred years since I encountered a she-dragon."

"What about the other girls? The sacrifices?"

"I never coupled with them. When I caressed them, their fears did not ease, not even when I showed them my human form. They did nothing but cringe and weep. What makes you different? This charm?" His fingernail tapped the bronze disk.

The amulet had done little enough for her, she thought, unless she gave it credit for keeping her alive. "A hundred years? I've heard my mother say men make—demands— almost every night. Are dragons different?"

He laughed and rocked his loins against hers. "No, we are not. When my hardness became unbearable, I relieved it by rubbing. Surely your kind—male and female—sometimes do the same?"

"Sometimes." She remembered the one night she had spied on Will as he flogged his cock until it spurted. She blushed hotter, thinking of her own solitary relief. A spark of renewed excitement overrode her exhaustion. She spread her legs and wrapped her arms around him.

The head of his cock probed her slit. He kissed her, his tongue thrusting in and out between her lips. His penis matched that motion, parting her damp folds, inserting the tip, and pulling back. Her legs opened wider. He penetrated beyond the entrance, but not far. She wiggled under him, eager for the quenching of the new fire he kindled, though her canal felt so tight she couldn't imagine how he could fit.

He nuzzled her hair. "Now. I cannot wait." Then he plunged deep inside her sheath.

A stab of pain impaled her. With a scream, she dug her nails into his back. "I am sorry for that," he whispered. "It could not be helped." Propped on his elbows to take his weight from her chest, he pumped in and out. A dull pain replaced the sharp one, yet when she locked her legs around his, she felt a delicious friction underneath the hurt. His eyes snared hers. "So hot—" he gasped. "Now—I must—"

He drove hard and fast, roared aloud, and arched his spine to rise above her. Throwing his head back, he thrust to the hilt and stiffened, his whole body quaking. She felt hot liquid spurt into her. Holding himself rigidly against her, he stayed that way for a long minute, before collapsing on top of her.

"Forgive me." He pulled out and lay on his side next to her, soothing her with long, slow strokes of his open palm. "That was the worst. It should not happen again."

Shuddering, she pressed her face to his shoulder, tears trickling from her eyes.

"Hush," he whispered. "From now on I will give you nothing but pleasure." Again he knelt between her thighs to lick the blood from her cleft. She trembled at the sensations that flooded her despite her soreness. Instead of pursuing her response to fulfillment, he returned to his former position, with her head on his chest, and began massaging her again. His hand stirred swirls of warmth as it coaxed the blood to her skin, making her flush all over. She caught herself rocking her hips in harmony with his caresses.

"Yes," he said, his breath ruffling her hair. "Claim your pleasure." His hand cupped her mound, while the thumb teased her "pearl." He kissed her forehead, ran his tongue along the curve of her cheek, and nibbled her earlobe. Every spot his lips touched felt tied with invisible cords to the sensitive bud that pulsed at each movement of his fingers. She rocked faster. He matched her speed, until she convulsed in ecstasy once more.

She went limp, panting for breath. To her surprise, she felt his cock hard against her side. Involuntarily her muscles tensed.

"Do not be afraid," he said. "I will not make that kind of—demand—until you have rested." A hint of laughter underlay the words. "But I do need to spend again." He rubbed the head of his pole on her thigh. His voice roughened with urgency. "Help me."

"How?"

He grasped her hand and wrapped it around his shaft. She squeezed. It felt like steel covered with satin. He moaned at the pressure of her fingers. "Yesss!"

Stroking up and down, she savored his rapid breaths and groans of need. The loose skin pulled back from the swollen, red tip. He moved her hand farther up the shaft and shoved the head of his cock into her palm. Her thumb found a narrow ridge that she stropped at the peak of each thrust.

She gazed into his eyes, alight with a ravenous glow. It looked like hunger, but now she knew she was in no danger of being killed and devoured. He rested one hand on her shoulder and stroked along her arm, then down her side and around to her breasts, skimming over each one in turn. The slow, gentle exploration contrasted oddly with the brisk jerks of his cock. She found the rhythm, sliding up and down in time with his quickening thrusts. When she began to squeeze and release every few seconds, deeper moans of pleasure rewarded her. She had power over him, she realized. She wasn't his helpless captive.

He guided her other hand to the sac between his thighs. Cupping it, she rubbed the silken hair around it and played with his balls. Her fingers discovered a thin ridge just behind the sac. When she pressed on it, he growled and dug his fingernails into her waist.

He humped faster, his teeth bared in a fierce rictus. Abruptly, he stiffened, his organ throbbing in her grasp, and hot fluid spurted from it. She clasped tighter, draining every drop, watching his eyes close and his face flush as he lost himself in his release.

He fell back on the cushions. The hand grasping her waist relaxed, and his eyes slowly opened. Groping among the silks, she found a square of linen that she used to wipe both of them dry.

Virid drew her into the circle of his arm, where she nestled against his hot, dry skin. "Thank you, my golden one." He gave her a lingering kiss; then they both lay still, gasping for breath.

A few minutes later he said, "Would you wish to return to your home?"

She rubbed her cheek against his shoulder. "I can't, even if you let me go. The elders would drive me out. They might even have me stoned."

"But if you could?"

"Of course I—" she started to answer. Then she stopped to consider. If she never went home, she would miss her parents and brothers, naturally. But she didn't think she would miss the drudgery of housework and farm labor. Nor did she regret losing the chance to marry one of the young men who could give her only a life of endless work and childbearing like her mother's. Not that Rowena would have had many suitors to choose from, with her meager dowry and her mother's dubious parentage. "I'm not sure."

"If you could have any life you dreamed of, what would you do?"

"Cut off my hair, disguise myself in boy's clothes, and run away to live as an outlaw in the greenwood." She laughed. "But that only works in ballads. I'd starve to death or get caught and hanged."

He hugged her close while drowsiness crept over her. "I would not allow any such fate to befall you."

Chapter Two

🙵

When Rowena woke up, she lay alone on the pile of cushions. She stretched, her muscles aching with an almost pleasant soreness. Daylight splashed through the cave entrance. She pulled herself to her feet and visited the pool chamber for a quick wash. Then she wrapped one of the silk sheets around her and walked to the portal.

The ravine yawned beneath her. Kneeling, she crept to the edge and looked down. A sheer drop met her eyes. She tossed a pebble into the air and watched it plummet to the distant ground. Lightheaded and queasy, she stood up and retreated to the entrance. Even if she wanted to escape, of which she wasn't sure anymore, climbing down that wall of rock would be impossible.

She saw Virid, in dragon form, flying toward the cave. He carried something in his front claws. Stepping back, she watched him land on the ledge. He clutched the body of a doe.

Rowena backed up farther while he deposited the deer in the middle of the great hall. For the first time she noticed a shallow depression in that part of the stone floor. The dragon scooped a bundle of sticks and logs from a stack at one side of the room. He blew a burst of flame from his mouth to ignite the firewood. Rowena jumped and let out a shriek. His glittering eyes turned toward her in what looked like amusement.

The flames leaped high, with the smoke curling up to the crevice in the ceiling. The fragrance of the burning wood tickled her nose. The dragon used a claw like a curved knife to slice off a haunch of deer and held it in the fire to roast it. Rowena sat cross-legged on a cushion, waiting until he decided the meat was cooked enough to give it to her. She wrapped it in a scrap of cloth and blew on it, her stomach grumbling with impatience. Charred on the outside and pink on the inside, the venison tasted better than anything she'd ever eaten. In her "other life," deer belonged to the Baron. Nobody of her class could hunt them without the risk of hanging as a poacher.

While eating, she worked up the courage to speak to him. "Do you stay in this cave all the time when you aren't hunting for game or snatching our herdsmen's sheep and cattle?" He showed no sign of anger, so she continued, "How do you spend your days?"

"I rest on my bed, after a night of flying over the mountain heights where human watchers will not disturb me with their shrieks of panic." He gestured toward the treasure trove. "I dream of past eons when my own kind thronged the earth. Sometimes I read."

She almost choked on a bite of meat. "You read?"

His jaws gaped in what might have been amusement. "Why does that surprise you? Have you never heard about the wisdom of dragons? Several of those chests are filled with books and scrolls in many human languages. You may read some if you wish."

"I can't read. Books are for priests and clerks." In fact, the only books she had ever seen were the leather-bound Bible chained to the lectern in the parish church and the volume used by the Baron's steward to record tax payments.

"I shall teach you, then."

She gazed into the fire, mulling over the strange notion of not only living with a winged reptile but having one for a tutor. "I do know some of my letters, enough to write my name. I learned from my grandmother." Grandmother would have taught her more, but Rowena's father had lashed out in anger and forbidden any such "useless dabbling."

His brows arched. "Indeed? How did she learn?"

"After her dragon let her go, or threw her out—she never explained which—she took up with a wandering minstrel. He also earned money as a scribe for people who needed letters written. He taught her to read and write."

"What brought her to settle in your village?"

"When they were passing through here, her man fell ill with a fever and died." Rowena tore off another strip of meat and chewed it, thinking over what little her grandmother had told her of that time. "She was almost ready to give birth to my mother. She bound herself as a farm laborer to earn her keep. When Mamma grew up and married, the Baron granted Grandmother a strip of land and a cottage next to my parents' holding." She gazed into the dragon's unblinking eyes. "You can't possibly be interested in an old woman's life story."

"But I am. I recognize the runes on the amulet."

Clutching the disk, she ran her fingers over the etchings. "What do they say?"

"The name of the original owner. Chrysargentophylax."

Her eyes widened. "You know him? Grandmother's dragon?"

His mouth stretched in what looked even more like a sardonic smile. "Of course. There are so few of us left now, it would be a wonder if I did not."

After the dragon devoured his share of the carcass, he flew outside to drop the remains into the ravine. He returned to Rowena and encircled her with his forefeet. Her heart raced at the touch of his claws, but she didn't fear them now.

"Why did you say your grandmother's amulet failed?"

"I told you." She leaned against his smooth, warm chest. "She claimed it would protect me from the dragon, but here I am. Your prisoner."

"My guest. My beloved." The words rumbled in her ears. "The amulet did protect you. It made me love you. And it revealed you as my true mate."

"What?" She wiggled around to look into his gem-like eyes.

"That is what I have sought in every maiden I took as tribute. A mate, one who can fulfill my passion and bear my young. Our kind become fewer every century. We are dying out." He pierced his own breast-scales with a claw tip. A trickle of blood, midnight blue instead of red, welled up.

"What are you doing?"

"Proving to you that you are my destined mate. Did you never ask your grandmother who sired her child?"

"She wouldn't say."

"I knew by the flavor of your essence," he said, "that you carry the bloodline of my own race. Your grandsire was a dragon. "

"But my mother's an ordinary woman."

"She never met one of us, did she? Her nature remained hidden. Here—taste." He guided her mouth to the puncture wound. "Awaken to your true self."

She licked the drops of blood. The fluid seared her tongue. It burned through it, racking her body with convulsions like a raging fever. She melted, dissolved, re-formed, expanded. Fangs sprouted in her jaws. Wings burst from her shoulders. A green mist swirled before her eyes. When it cleared, she looked down to find the floor far below and her chest and legs gleaming with blue-green scales. The thong around her neck had snapped. She picked up the amulet and placed it on the treasure heap. She no longer needed protection.

A fire smoldered in the pit of her stomach. Her companion's name bubbled into her head like sparkling wine. She spoke it with a burst of flame: "Viridiseffulgentissimus."

"Rowenaureadulcima," he crooned. Smoke billowed from his jaws. Viridiseffulgentissimus rubbed his fearsome head against hers. "My mate. My beloved. Fly with me."

She slithered to the exit and perched on the ledge with her wings spread. "What did you call me?"

"That name reflects only one facet of your true self. As you grow, you will gain others. And you will learn to speak all of mine."

He leaped into the air. Gathering her courage, she launched herself after him. A gust of wind swept under her wings. She soared high after her mate, with the wind of their flight howling in her ears. They flew straight toward the early morning sun, but its glare caused no pain to her newly keen eyes. The vast, clear blue of the sky beckoned. Within minutes they reached a height that seemed halfway to the gates of Heaven.

This is my adventure!

Gliding on air currents, she gazed down at fields and forests so distant that the patches of green looked like a child's drawing and the widely scattered clusters of houses like toy blocks.

"Do not fly low over towns," her mate rumbled. "The fools would shoot arrows at us."

He wheeled around and headed for the higher mountains in the distance. She kept pace, her wings beating tirelessly. The thin, cold air tasted like sparkling wine. Heated by the sun, the fire in her entrails flared to a burst of blue and green smoke that shot from her maw in a column the length of her body.

The heat spread through her veins and transformed to molten sweetness in the cleft beneath her tail. Her mate flew circles around her and ejected a matching gout of smoke. A quick glance showed her the crimson of his erect shaft against his belly.

Suddenly, he flew out of sight. She scarcely had a second to realize he was above her before he swooped down and fastened his jaws in her neck.

A shock went through her, making her inner muscles clench. With a shriek of impatience, she coiled her serpentine tail out of the way. All four of his legs wrapped around her torso, and his talons dug into her scales. The piercing of his claws made her quiver with eagerness. The underside of his wings swept the top of hers. With each stroke, the friction between the membranes shot sparks of excitement along her spine.

His fangs penetrated the scales at the nape of her neck, not quite hard enough to hurt, a fierce sting that quivered on the edge of pain. A subtle forward shift of his weight signaled his intention to start downward. Together they folded their wings and dove toward the earth. At the same instant, his pole surged into her. Her sheath rippled around him. Their hurtling descent sharpened the sensation until she almost blacked out from the exquisite blend of pleasure and near-pain. Lightning flashed behind her eyelids.

His shaft slid in and out, gliding along the liquid heat inside her. She clenched her inner muscles, trapping him. The angle of their dive steepened, forcing his cock to plunge into her up to the root. The fullness of his balls pressed against her cleft. Shuddering in release, she felt his molten seed spurt into her depths.

Just as the ground rushed toward them, he opened his wings and lofted both himself and her skyward. In the fading convulsions of ecstasy, she threw her head back and roared a tower of flame. His fire leaped to meld with hers.

Breaking their embrace, they flew toward the mountains again. "What would you wish now, my beloved?" he said.

"Fly higher!"

So they did.

Chapter Three

🐉

At the next dawn, Rowena woke restored to woman-shape, once more alone on the pile of silks. For a moment she imagined the past two days might have been a fever dream, a delirium born of her terror at being staked out for a monster. When she came fully awake, though, she realized it had all happened as she remembered, the dragon's lovemaking and her own transformation. At the sight of her grandmother's amulet, he had suspected Rowena of dragon ancestry. A taste of her blood had confirmed that belief. And one searing drop of his blood on her tongue had wakened her dragon nature and given her the power to change her form. After a day of soaring flight, she had returned to the lair exhausted.

She gazed at the pearlescent glow of the cave walls and the pile of gems and coins. A scent like charred pine boughs prickled her nose. The draft from the crevice high overhead cooled the sheen of sweat on her bare arms. "Virid—" The dragon was nowhere to be seen. She tried to speak his full name, but she discovered she couldn't manage it with her human mind and tongue.

He sought a mate, he'd said, a female to bear his young. Sitting up and allowing the cloth to slide off her naked body, Rowena ran her fingers through her tangled hair. *Do I want to live the rest of my life in a cave as a dragon's mate?* Now that she knew her own true nature, she had choices. A woman couldn't climb down the ravine, but a she-dragon could fly away. Still musing over the strangeness of her new life, she walked to the bathing chamber. Her thighs and the cleft between them were sore but not truly painful. The cave felt less chilly to her today. Perhaps the stirring of her dragon blood bestowed inner heat that kept her warm. While splashing in the bathing pool, she recalled Virid's ardor and his words of love. What did love mean to a creature so far from human, even if he could take man-shape at will? True, he had ravished her with his lovemaking. Her quim tingled at the thought. Yet could they share a life based on carnal delights alone?

After drying herself, she rummaged in the chests near the treasure hoard. She found a linen undertunic and green kirtle that fit her well enough. She left her feet bare. With a tortoiseshell comb, she worked the knots out of her hair, then plaited it into a single braid. She drank water from another spring she found in a side niche and ate two peaches to soothe the grumbling of her stomach. Since they hadn't made her sick the last time, she decided raw fruit must be safe to eat, after all. Just as she tossed the second peach pit off the edge of the precipice, Virid came swooping toward the cave with a pair of rabbits in his claws. His wingspread overshadowed her, making her breath catch in her chest. She had momentarily forgotten how huge his dragon body loomed. *He vowed not to harm me,* she reminded herself. She backed up to let him enter.

"You human folk need to eat so often," he rumbled. "A good meal fills me for days." Depositing the rabbits in the fire pit, he skinned them with his claws and then roasted them with his flame breath. "Eat quickly, my precious one. Regain your strength so we can mate again." His tongue snaked around her neck and insinuated itself down her bodice between her breasts.

Waves of fire and ice rippled through her. "Again?" Her breath caught in her throat. "From what I've heard from married women, human men can't have that many cockstands in two days. Don't you ever grow tired of fucking?" She blushed at the crude word that slipped out, but for a creature more vigorous than any stallion, it seemed fitting.

"I cannot say, since it has been so long since I—fucked." Humor tinged his voice, as if her blush amused him. "We dragons have become so few that we encounter our own kind very seldom. It is part of our nature to mate hard and often when the chance arises. Otherwise we would not beget enough offspring to preserve our race."

His voice lowered to a growl. "I need to fuck you now. The meat will take some time to cool anyway." He hooked a claw in her bodice. "Disrobe at once."

His imperious tone roused indignation that fought with the excitement in the pit of her stomach. "What am I, your mate or your slave?"

He reared onto his hind legs, his jaws gaping and his pole standing at full erection. Rowena drew back, a tremor coursing through her. *He can't kill me,* she reassured herself. *Not if he thinks I am his true mate.*

"Forgive me, my golden treasure." He shrank and shimmered into human form. " I do not mean to frighten you. Blame the strength of my ardor."

He held out his arms. Hesitantly, she stepped into the circle of his embrace. One of his hands rubbed the center of her back like a man gentling a skittish mare. The other lifted her braid and let it slide through his fingers. She felt him picking apart the entwined locks.

"What are you doing?" she murmured. His hand massaging her through the fabric of the kirtle sent ripples of sensation chasing each other down her spine. His touch drained away her fear.

"I want to see and touch it unbound." When he finished unbraiding her hair, he let it cascade through his fingers. "Like a waterfall of molten gold." He raised a few strands to his face and inhaled. "Your scent is delicious."

"I like yours, too." With her head leaning on his chest, Virid's aroma of spices and pine boughs tickled her nose. She rubbed her cheek against the smooth layer of tiny scales.

With a deep-pitched chuckle, he ran his fingers through her hair again and again, letting it trickle through his loose grasp like the waterfall he'd mentioned. Young Will Baker had never taken the time for such caresses. Most often, he had groped her between her legs with the first kiss. Rowena sighed and snuggled tighter against Virid, whose upstanding cock pressed hard on her lower abdomen.

Meanwhile, he continued stroking her back, moving lower little by little. She tilted her head to gaze into his smoldering eyes. She put her own hand on his chest, fascinated by the smoothness of the tiny scales. When she shifted her fingers to brush his right nipple, the tip hardened like a pebble. He drew in a hissing breath, and his eyes widened. His hand crept down her spine until he gathered up her skirt, and his palm splayed over her arse. He rubbed the twin globes in slow circles. Moisture pooled between her legs. Planting her feet farther apart, she pressed against him to bring her wet folds in contact with the curve of his hip. The cloth tucked between them made her moan in frustration.

Virid looked down at her with a smile that showed the points of his sharp teeth. "You seem uncomfortable."

The teasing tone emboldened her. She squirmed, trying to fit his cock into the triangle at the apex of her legs. Still smiling, he shifted to evade her efforts. She stood on tiptoe and nipped his shoulder. Again he hissed. His arms tightened around her. "Here's a mortal biting a dragon! Why such fierceness?"

"I need more. Please."

"Do you desire me?" he said, lowering his head to nuzzle the top of hers.

A blush suffused her. "You know I do."

"You are no longer afraid?" With the hand under her skirt, he clasped her bare bottom. One of his fingers slid between her buttocks and probed the crack.

She gasped. A fresh gush of liquid flooded her cleft. "No. I'm not afraid now." She paused to consider the question. Their embrace seemed to demand honesty. "Not right this moment. I was a little while ago."

"What changed?"

"This." She stretched her legs and again tried to rub against his shaft through the bunched fabric of her kirtle. "If you want me, I know you won't hurt me. And I want you too much to fear your touch." Did she really dare to say these things to a creature not even human?

"I have already vowed I would never harm you. I do not want to cause you pain. Have you recovered from our last coupling?" His voice, no longer teasing, roughened with desire.

"Yes," she breathed. Her heart raced. She felt lightheaded. The traces of soreness between her legs faded to nothing when his fingers crept from behind into her wet quim. She automatically moved her thighs apart to give him easier access. A growl in his chest and the twitching of his cock assured her he felt the same urgency. He thrust one finger inside her while others played with her damp curls and teased her bud. It felt unbearably swollen and tight. Her sheath squeezed his finger, but she needed more. "Please—"

"Tell me what you want."

"Frig me!"

He strummed her bud. She clung to him and rocked back and forth, his cock bouncing against her stomach. He watched her face, as if savoring her passion.

"Do the same for me," he said hoarsely.

She gripped his shaft and pumped up and down. His jaws clenched, and his breath became as rapid and shallow as hers. The bolts of pleasure shooting through her made her movements erratic, but he made no complaint about the way the pattern of her strokes turned into a series of random jerks and squeezes. Her whole consciousness narrowed to the vibrations between her thighs. Her bud quivered, and he rubbed even faster. She spent in ever-widening ripples of exquisite sensation.

"Now!" he growled. He spun her around and pushed her face down onto the cushions. Still trembling with her release, she didn't resist. Virid hiked up her skirt, shoved her knees apart, and rammed his cock into her slick canal. This time it felt tight but not painful. Her whole body shook with the force of his thrust. He paused at full depth, grasping her buttocks. She felt the muscles of his thighs quivering.

"Don't stop!" Her fists closed on the cushion under her, and she bit into a fold of the silk. His shaft slid out of her, inch by inch, then slowly penetrated to the root again. "Faster," she whimpered.

"Give me your clitoris."

"My what?" she gasped.

"This." One of his hands burrowed between her thighs and found the aching bud. "It means a little hill in the Greek tongue. The peak of your passion." He rubbed vigorously while pounding into her. She thrust back and forth with him, struggling to find the rhythm.

He quickened his pace. She felt his hot breath on the back of her neck, sending waves of heat and cold down her spine. His other hand cupped her breast. "Now, my love!"

His fingers danced faster over her clitoris. He thrust into her deeper than she had imagined he could. Her flesh pulsed in harmony with the tremors of his taut muscles. She was flying higher — higher —

The molten heat of his seed shot into her. Her arms and legs stiffened. Her upper body rose off the cushion, her back arched, and she cried out in a shattering culmination.

Exhausted, she lay with her face buried in the silk until Virid gently rolled her over. With her eyes closed, she felt him clean her thighs with a cool, damp cloth and pat them dry with another. He rearranged her clothes and took her by the hand. Opening her eyes, she gazed into the emerald glow of his. No, she did not fear him now. He'd called her "love." While she couldn't be sure what the word meant to him, it was clear that he meant to cherish her.

"Come to the fire and eat, my golden one. You need plenty of food to nourish the babe we shall conceive."

Putting the uneasy notion of mothering a dragon child out of her mind, she let him lead her to the meat he had seared, now comfortably warm. Her stomach cramped with hunger at the odor. She eagerly bit into the haunch he sliced off for her.

A few minutes later, with the sharpness of both lust and hunger blunted, she managed to collect her thoughts enough to speak. Munching a leg of roast rabbit, she waved at the scattered chests and caskets near the treasure heap. "What's in those besides books, clothes, and bolts of cloth? More jewels?"

"Not all of them. When you finish your meal, I will show you."

After eating her fill of the meat, she washed in a basin of water from the spring and followed Virid to the nearest casket. He opened it to display a pile of loose pearls— hundreds, even more than were sewn on the Baroness' festival gown. Rowena gasped and ran her fingers through them. The pearls slid over her skin like a cool stream.

"Yes, they have beauty," Virid said, "but why human folk ascribe such special value to gems and shiny metals, I have never understood. These other treasures are equally precious." He opened a larger chest. Stacks of rolled-up scrolls filled it. "Some of these are a thousand years old, in languages you have never heard of."

She skimmed a fingertip along the edge of one parchment roll. Ancient tongues seemed as mysterious as magic to her, since she could not even read her own language. "Can you read them?"

"Some. I have had many centuries to learn."

Shivering at this fresh mention of his vast age, Rowena decided not to ask for a precise number. How could such a creature view her as more than a temporary amusement, the way a caged sparrow might be for a human captor in the brief time before its death? Or did the wakening of her dragon blood mean she, too, would have a lifespan like Virid's? She wasn't sure which prospect troubled her more.

He showed her a chest full of bound books—codexes, he called them. "Soon I will teach you to read, if you wish it." Another chest held swords and daggers wrapped in oiled cloth to preserve them from rust. Bolts of silk and linen filled other boxes, along with luxurious garments in green, blue, gold, and scarlet, decorated with delicate embroidery, dazzling in contrast to the drab russet she'd worn all her life. Some of the robes looked exotically different from the clothes the Baron's family wore. Perhaps they came from distant countries.

"You haven't always lived here, have you?" she said. She vaguely remembered the grandsires of her village mentioning a time before the dragon had shadowed their lives.

"Only for about fifty years. No matter how pleasant a lair is, I cannot keep it forever. I must move from place to place until human memories fade, and I can return to a former home."

From the chest he picked out a cloak lined with fur. She had never seen the like, even on the Baron or his lady. Virid draped it around her shoulders. "You will need this if you feel chilled."

"I don't, but I like it anyway." She ran her fingers over the fur lining, smoother and softer than any kitten or downy chick.

He showed her an alcove with shelves carved into the rock wall. Glass vials of different colors lined the shelves. "Distilled nectar of poppies," he said, holding up one of several red bottles, "for the relief of pain and the invocation of sleep. I have used it to calm some of my tribute maidens. I am pleased that your courage makes it unnecessary."

Although chilled by the image of young women drugged into a stupor for the dragon's convenience, she also felt a flush of pleasure. No one had ever credited her with courage before. "What about the other bottles?"

He touched a vial of green glass. "Tincture of willow bark for the cooling of fevers." Then one of violet. "These hold a cordial to stop coughing. Some of my guests have become ill from the coolness of my lair." Finally he picked up a blue bottle, one of only two. "All the others come from the skill of apothecaries. This one is true magic, a potion of healing. That is why I have so little of it."

She looked over his strong, smooth-muscled body. "Why would you ever need healing?"

With a dry laugh, he said, "Knights and wizards sometimes dare to attack me, and sometimes they succeed. I have suffered enough wounds to be glad of this magic." Taking her hand in his cool grasp, he led her to another alcove, packed with barrels and casks of various sizes. "Mead, wines from Burgundy and Italy, and a fiery liquor made by the Hibernians across the sea. They call it water of life."

Dazed by the sheer profusion of precious objects, Rowena freed her hand from his and sank onto the cushions again, rubbing her temples to quiet the turmoil of her thoughts. "Why do you have all these things? What use are they to you?"

"It is the nature of dragons to hoard wealth of all kinds. Some treasures I gathered on my own, but many of these objects were given to me as tribute by folk in the regions where I lived before I settled here." He sat cross-legged beside her.

"To bribe you not to eat their daughters?"

"I have told you, I do not eat human flesh. At least, except during times of desperate starvation. A sheep or cow or even a deer tastes much better." A laugh as cold as polished silver rippled from him. "Not that my human neighbors needed to know that. Yes, they lavished gifts on me to protect themselves from my appetite."

His casual dismissal of human fears sparked anger in Rowena. "You don't deny you've killed people sometimes, do you?"

He shook his head with obvious impatience. "Your kind are my natural prey. When human men have dared to strike at me with their crude weapons, of course I have slain them."

His tone chilled her. She wanted no reminder that in normal circumstances he would see her only as "prey" or, at best, a minor nuisance infesting the landscape.

Clearly noticing the way she shrank from him, he pulled her into his arms and stroked her hair. Against her will, she melted in the warmth of his embrace. "Come, my sweet, these things happened long ago. Now I shall leave all human folk unmolested for your sake. Put the past out of your thoughts, and drink with me."

From one of the open chests he took a pair of silver goblets, inlaid with blue stones. "Turquoise," he said. He filled each cup from a small cask of what he had called "water of life." "Drink carefully," he said, handing her a cup.

The liquid looked as clear as water but had a strong aroma. She took a tentative sip. The liquor seared down her throat and settled in her stomach like a hot coal. With a sputtering cough, she said, "It—burns."

"Take it slowly, and you will come to enjoy it." Taking her hand, he drew her onto the cushions. The cloak slid off as she lay down. "Try it this way." He siphoned a bit of his drink into his mouth, then cradled her head in his hand and kissed her.

A few drops of the liquor seeped between her lips. Startled, she parted them to let the rest of the mouthful trickle in. The warmth of Virid's tongue and his cinnamon-like flavor softened the sting of the drink. When she swallowed, the liquid fire again flowed through her throat and chest to the pit of her stomach. Its heat radiated through her body to ignite a fresh stirring between her legs.

"Better?" He took another sip and fed it to her the same way, pausing after she swallowed to nibble the sides of her mouth.

Sighing, she wrapped her arms around his neck and pulled him close for a deeper kiss. When she had to stop for breath, he transferred another portion of water of life from his mouth to hers.

"Now you can surely drink from the goblet," he said. He drained his own cup and placed hers in her hand.

With care, she tried a sip. It did go down more smoothly now. Little by little, she emptied the cup. As soon as she finished, Virid kissed her again. Her eyes drifted shut while the tip of his tongue explored the corners of her mouth, the inside of her lips, the edge of her teeth. She felt dizzy.

Cool air replaced the warmth of Virid's body. She opened her eyes to see him drawing another draft of liquor into each of the goblets. He nestled into the cushions with her once more and pressed a cup into her hand. When he drained his, she followed his example. She didn't mind the burning at all now. Her head seemed to float. From her lax grip the goblet rolled onto the floor.

Virid set down his empty goblet and shifted his body to cover hers. Through her skirt, she felt his hardening cock. He cupped her breast through her bodice. A heavy ache spread from her breasts to her quim. His open palm brushed the stiff nipple.

"Want it off," she said, squirming under him. The nipple rubbed tantalizingly against the cloth.

"What?" he said with a feral smile.

She fumbled with the ribbons at her neck. He untied them, reached for the hem of the kirtle, and helped her shrug out of the garment. The linen undertunic still covered the parts of her body she yearned for him to touch. "And this," she said, tugging the smock upward.

He reached under it to fondle her triangle of hair. The burning between her legs increased. "Can I not swive you in your shift?"

His teasing tone maddened her. "Don't want it on." She sat up, dislodging his hand, and peeled off the undergarment. Her head and stomach lurched. Giggling, she flopped down on the pillows. "Now you can touch me the right way."

"This way?" He covered her mount of Venus again, while he bent over her to flick each nipple with his tongue. When she moaned and arched her back, he lapped one nipple in a rhythm that made her skin prickle with delicious chills in contrast to the fire in her stomach and between her thighs.

His fingertip barely touched her bud, swollen so tightly she felt it might burst. She undulated her hips. Lifting his head, Virid gazed into her half-closed eyes. "Am I not doing it the right way?"

"Don't stop licking!"

He gave the opposite nipple a light flick of his tongue. "Is that all you want?"

"You know what I want." She pressed his hand into her mound. "It burns. Frig me again." A hot blush spread over her bare skin. She had certainly never talked to Will this way. But surely mating with a dragon had different rules.

At once Virid claimed her breast with his mouth once more, and his fingers danced over her quim. Two of them probed inside her, while another strummed her bud. Fire seemed to flood her veins. Her bud and her sheath pulsed like another heartbeat. She screamed, clutched Virid's shoulders, and dug her nails into his flesh.

Lost in a whirlpool of sensation, she became dimly aware that his cock still pressed against her thigh. "Come in!" she gasped. At once he plunged inside. The world spun around her. The cave floor seemed to tilt as if spilling her into empty space. Caught in his arms, she found herself rolling over. She crouched on top of him, while he thrust upward, impaling her on his pole. She rode him, her nails still scoring his shoulders and chest. One final thrust shot his fire into her. She cried out, convulsed in ecstasy, and collapsed upon him.

Panting, she moved sideways to take her full weight off his chest. "I never expected this," she said when she caught her breath. "Such rapture. And so many times." She ran her hand over the scratches she had inflicted. They oozed bluish blood instead of red. Her head still swimming, she rested it on his shoulder while he lay supine against the pillows.

"Remember, my treasure," he murmured, "the more often we mate, the sooner our child will be conceived."

Did she want that result? Her stomach knotted with anxiety at the thought of bearing any child in this strange nursery, much less a babe that most people would call a monster. Rather than anger Virid by voicing these doubts, she asked the question uppermost in her mind. "If I get with child, will it be human or dragon?"

"I know the answer to that no more than you. Such crossbreeds are matters of legend, not living memory. Your grandmother bore a human-appearing child, and the dragon heritage hid in your mother's blood until it woke in yours."

"Then shouldn't my baby, if I have one, look human, too?" In the back of her mind lurked the thought that if she became unhappy with Virid, she could take her child and flee to some distant town, as her grandmother had. Or, if none would accept her, she might become an outlaw in the greenwood, as she'd fancied in her girlhood. With dragon powers, she could feed and protect herself and her baby.

"Not necessarily. Your grandam was entirely human, so her offspring was only half draconic. Because you come from a part-dragon bloodline, our young might be a wyrmling, or perhaps midway between wyrmling and human babe."

"What's a wyrmling?" she asked drowsily.

"A dragonet, a child of our kind."

Still lightheaded from the drink, she rubbed her eyes, trying to keep alert long enough to ask the question weighing on her heart. "I wish I could talk to Grandmother. If she would tell me what really happened to her while she lived with her dragon, maybe I would know better what to expect."

A growl rumbled in Virid's chest. "What truths could she offer that I cannot? In any case, you will never see her again, so put that notion out of your mind."

Chapter Four

ॐ

Rowena lifted her head to gaze into his jewel-green eyes. "But I *could* see her. I could fly there and visit in secret. No one else would have to know, but at least I could show my family I'm alive, so they wouldn't grieve."

"Stop being a fool!" He gave her a brisk shake, then drew her into such a tight embrace that she could hardly breathe. "You told me what your grandam's own people did to her. I will not allow you to risk your life."

"My life?" She squirmed until he relaxed his hold. "Now you're the one talking like a fool. Even if my neighbors caught me, they wouldn't hurt me. They would only throw me out. And I would have a chance to help my parents, too. I could bring them a little of the treasure."

He glowered at her. "You show remarkable generosity with my wealth."

She glared back at him. "You could easily spare a handful of coins and a few small gems. You'd never notice the lack. Besides, if I'm your mate instead of your captive, isn't it my wealth, too?"

"That is irrelevant. What do you suppose would happen to your parents if they tried to spend coins from an unknown source? What would your Baron do in such a case?"

Though she realized he had a valid point, she didn't want to admit defeat. "We could think of a way around that problem. If only I could see them once—"

"Enough! Stop this nonsense, or I will have to silence you."

A shiver went through her at the blaze of anger in his eyes. She raised her chin, trying to look unafraid. "How?"

"Thus." Gripping her head in both hands, he covered her mouth with his. Her lips parted involuntarily. His tongue teased hers, and she explored his lips while tasting his incense-tinged breath. Waves of heat and cold swept over her.

After a long, languid kiss, he released her, eased her onto the cushions, and covered her with a silken sheet. "Rest, my treasure. After drinking so deeply, I cannot hold this shape much longer." He walked over to the treasure pile and reclined on it. Once again the air around him shimmered, and he returned to his dragon form. Copper and silver clinked under his weight. Stretching out his serpentine neck, he closed his eyes and sank into sleep.

Standing up, Rowena staggered with vertigo. Her head still reeled from the liquor. She giggled, then clapped a hand over her mouth. Virid showed no sign of being disturbed by the noise. With exaggerated care, she tiptoed over to his motionless bulk, leaning on the wall for support when she stumbled. His chest expanded and deflated in the slow rhythm of sleep. Wisps of smoke curled from his nostrils with each breath. She laid a hand on his scaly side. No reaction.

The depth of his slumber sparked an idea. *I don't need his permission to visit home. I can fly there and back before he ever wakes up.*

Naked, she fumbled her way to the portal. She blinked and rubbed her eyes until they adjusted to the glare of the sun. When she drew a deep breath and visualized her body swelling into dragon shape, a spasm of doubt racked her. Could she transform without her mate's help? Did the magic really flow in her blood, or had he worked the change through his power?

Shaking off her qualms, she closed her eyes and groped for the core of fire at her heart. She conjured up the image of her other self, huge, winged, iridescent, armed with fierce teeth and claws. Her dragon nature flared up like a torch bursting into flame. When she opened her eyes, the aquamarine wings lay folded along her sides, and her hands had become talons.

The landscape spread out below her. Her newly keen eyes picked out her home village in the distance. For a moment the sheer drop into the ravine made her queasy. Suppose she jumped into the void and discovered she couldn't fly without Viridiseffulgentissimus beside her?

Of course I can. I changed without help, didn't I? Dragon power was part of her nature. He had said so himself.

She crept to the ledge and teetered on the rim of it. Only here could she unfold her wings to their full span. She tried an experimental flap, enjoying the cool breeze her motion stirred. Another giggle burbled in her throat, a sound that came out as a low growl from her fanged jaws. She leaped off the ledge.

Wind rushed up to meet her. She lurched sideways and flapped frantically to right herself. Raising her head, she hurtled upward through turbulent air. Too high, too fast. She struggled to level off and rolled almost completely over. Her head reeled.

When she managed to force her flight under control, she had cleared the ravine and was soaring in the direction of the village. On a hilltop to her left, she glimpsed the Baron's square-towered castle. An urge seized her to swoop over the keep and disgorge flame on the lord's guardsmen, those men who had dragged her to the tree of sacrifice and tied her there as a feast for a monster. She restrained herself, knowing her mate would not approve of provoking them.

She wobbled with dizziness whenever she turned or banked. The liquor hadn't worn off, she realized. Maybe she had better not try to visit her family this time. She would settle for a quick glimpse of her home and come back another day, when she wasn't befuddled with drink and had learned to use her wings more smoothly.

Soon she caught sight of the stream that flowed through town and drove the mill wheel. She followed the watercourse through the gradually thinning forest toward the village. When she approached near enough to distinguish one building from another, she suddenly recalled the dragon's warning against flying too low. She couldn't let herself be seen. She launched herself skyward in a series of awkward jerks and irregular wing flaps. *I must look like a barnyard goose pretending to be a swan,* she thought. Her mate would be ashamed of her clumsiness.

Rising in a tight spiral, she circled high above the village. Was she high enough that anyone who happened to glance up would mistake her for a hawk? Her dragon eyes saw so much more sharply than her human sight that she couldn't judge distance by her own view of the landscape below. She picked out the village square, with the well and the small, stone church. The common croplands, strips of various shades of green and yellow, surrounded the central cluster of cottages with their sheds and outbuildings. She could see people and animals moving around the fields and kitchen gardens.

After a few minutes to get her bearings, she identified the small plot held by her parents. In the open space between the two-room, thatch-roofed house and the chicken coop, a plump, brown-haired woman bent over a washtub.

Mamma! Rowena almost dove toward the ground to show herself. Just in time, she checked her dive and spiraled upward again. Did she want to make her mother drop dead from terror? If she wanted to greet her parents she would have to take human form.

Why not? Her earlier resolution to keep out of sight wavered. What harm would it do to find a hiding place where she could change shape, then slink around the outskirts of town to her parents' cottage? She would stay for only a few minutes, just long enough to reassure them of her survival. Nobody else had to see her.

She had spent several minutes looking for a good landing spot before sense prevailed again. Did she plan to walk up to her mother stark naked? A meeting would require better preparation, including a set of clothes to wear while in her woman shape.

Still, she lingered over the cottage a while longer, watching her mother rinse the linens and drape them over the hedge to dry, with "help" from one of the little boys. Rowena's flight was becoming smoother. Maybe the drink's effect was fading, for her elation had evaporated. The glimpse of home only made clear to her how irrevocably she had been torn away from it. She descended a little lower for one last look. For the first time she noticed a small figure wrapped in a blanket in the shelter of the doorway. Although the shadow of the house impeded her view, she decided the person had to be her youngest brother, four-year-old Harold.

Why was he lying there in broad daylight? Was he sick? If she met her mother face to face, she could find out what was wrong. Again the impossibility of that meeting forced itself upon her. Sadness clogged her throat. No, she certainly couldn't let her family see her this way.

Veering away, she headed back toward the stream. The millpond reflected the midsummer sun. She saw no one near the mill. Probably the miller was at work inside or dealing with one of the lord's tenants who had come to have grain ground into flour. Rowena thought about the times she had examined her own reflection in the pond's surface. She realized she hadn't seen her dragon face yet. Surely it would be safe to land for just a minute.

Flapping to slow her descent, she sank to the earth. The humid warmth of the summer day enveloped her. The upper air had been refreshingly cool in comparison. Her nostrils flared at the scents of grass, soil, water, and chaff. Another smell permeated the atmosphere too, the odor of human flesh and sweat clinging to the manmade structures that surrounded her. With her long tail dragging on the turf, she crawled to the verge of the pond between a pair of drooping willow trees.

Large, gleaming eyes stared back at her from the water's surface. Iridescent scales armored her neck. A crest stood up on the top of her head. She opened her mouth, gaping almost as wide as her mate's. Teeth like daggers, made for stabbing and rending, lined her jaws. Any human being she tried to greet with that smile would flee in horror — or draw a sword and attack her. Hot tears dropped from her eyes and hissed in the water.

A sound penetrated her misery, the noise of a door slamming on the other side of the mill. The miller's voice called a farewell. His footsteps then tramped across the floor in Rowena's direction. If he emerged on the water side of the building, he would come face to face with her.

She backed away from the pond, shredding the turf with her claws. When she started to spread her wings, they brushed the branches of the trees on either side. She needed more room. The miller's steps were coming closer. She scrabbled backward, breathing hard in rising fear. Smoke puffed from her nose and wide-open mouth. After a few seconds of flailing between the trees, she reached the open space where she had landed.

She flexed her legs to push off from the ground. For an instant she feared she would only sink to earth again, but the frantic beating of her wings raised her from the ground. Just as she straightened out and cleared the treetops, the miller stepped outside. He looked up.

She settled into a steady glide. While fleeing skyward as fast as her new flight skills allowed, she glimpsed the miller staring after her with his mouth open in shock, fortunately too stunned to scream. *He saw me! He'll tell the whole village he saw a dragon!* What would they do when they heard of a dragon's invasion outside the customary Midsummer Eve encounter?

She reminded herself that the tenant farmers and craftsmen of the town, or even the Baron with his men at arms, could pose no real threat. Even if they knew the location of the dragon's lair, they had no way to climb up to the cave without being struck down long before reaching the entrance. The pounding of her heart slowed. She breathed deeply of the cool air that blew into her face as she flew. It refreshed her after the humidity and human scents on the ground.

A distant flying shape caught her eye. When it drew near at a speed much faster than hers, she recognized the huge, blue-green body and giant wingspread. Viridiseffulgentissimus hurtled toward her, flame spouting from his maw. It shot past her, only a few wingspans away. She felt the heat on her flank. She dodged, and he followed, pacing her almost close enough to touch wingtips.

"Faster!" he roared at her in a voice like thunder. "To the lair! Fly!" His anger rushed over her like a storm. He surged ahead. She flew in his wake, struggling to keep her balance in the wind churned up by the beat of his wings.

Scant minutes seemed to pass before they reached the cave, a much quicker flight than she'd managed on her own.

Viridiseffulgentissimus glided inside first, then turned to watch her clumsy landing. Her chest burned from her labored breathing. The back muscles that flexed her wings ached. The moment she collapsed onto the cave's floor, she flowed from dragon shape into her human body. On hands and knees, she looked up at the male dragon who loomed over her with his fangs bared. She trembled at the thought that he could kill her with a single blast of fire. She would not beg for mercy, though. She waited, motionless.

Instead of attacking, he changed to his man shape, which still towered over her. "You witless child!" he hissed. "Why did you defy me? Do you consider your life so worthless?"

"I only wanted one look at my home! What's the harm in that?"

"What harm?" He seized her arm in a painful grip and yanked her to her feet. "Suppose they had captured you? As it is, you were spotted. You cannot deny that. I saw that man watching your flight."

"So?" She tried to pull her arm free, but she couldn't match his strength. "What can he possibly do, besides tell his neighbors a dragon landed by the millpond?"

Virid dragged her to the cushions and flung her onto her back. "And your village elders will report to the Baron, will they not? What do you suppose he will do?" He sank to his knees beside Rowena, grabbed her shoulders, and shook her. "Damnation, woman, when I woke and found you gone, my heart froze."

Her eyes stung with tears from the shaking. She rubbed them away. "Why?"

"Why?" He stared at her as if she'd gone mad. "Because I thought you might have fled from me. Or else you had done some idiotic trick to put yourself in mortal danger. Either way, I feared I had lost you."

Did he truly care about losing her? Or only that he might have to go to the trouble of finding another female to bear his young? Rowena put the question out of her mind when he drew her into a tight embrace and stroked her hair.

"Beloved, my anger arose from fear for your safety." His heat enveloped her, and his heartbeat pounded in her ears.

"But what is there to be afraid of? You're an ancient dragon, and they're only human."

"Listen carefully and believe me this time." His hand skimmed over her head, down her back, and up again in a soothing rhythm that melted away her aches. "I have a bargain with your Baron. Once a year, the folk of his holdings offer me a woman as tribute. In exchange, I leave them alone, aside from snatching an occasional beast from their flocks and herds if the game becomes scarce. Because your lord knows he can trust me not to prey on his subjects, he sends no swordsmen or archers in search of my lair. What will he do if he decides he can no longer trust that bargain?"

Rowena tilted her head to gaze into his emerald eyes. "What do you mean?"

"The miller saw you. A dragon in an inhabited place, and not on Midsummer Eve. I doubt your people can tell one dragon from another. They only know they may be in danger, danger the tribute was supposed to prevent."

It still seemed to her that Virid was becoming alarmed over nothing. "But what could they *do*? Even if they knew where this cave is and could get up here somehow, surely you're more powerful than any of the Baron's fighting men."

"Let me show you something." He strode across the chamber and opened a chest full of books. He brought back to the sleeping alcove a leather-bound volume with gold on the edges of the leaves. Rowena sat up, hugging her knees to her chest and looking over his shoulder while he flipped through the pages. He turned to a picture of a red dragon with a snakelike head belching lurid flames. A man in armor stood astride its body and stabbed a lance into the dragon's belly, from which a fountain of blood spurted.

Virid pointed to the words that accompanied the illustration. "I must teach you to read this writing. It is in the Latin tongue and tells of Saint Georgius, renowned for the slaying of dragons."

Rowena's stomach turned queasy at the vivid picture of the gory wound. "Where did this happen? How long ago?"

"No one knows. It is a legend of great antiquity."

"Well, then, maybe it never happened at all. Maybe it's no more than a tale for the fireside." She reached over Virid's forearm to close the book, eager to get the picture out of sight and mind.

"Such tales often inspire action. Many a knight dreams of imitating this hero's deeds."

She shook her head impatiently. "But there aren't any such knights in our Baron's domain. I have seen his men at arms. They don't look like heroes of ancient legend. They wear mail coats and short swords, except those who carry bows. I can hardly imagine any of them challenging you."

Baring his teeth in a predator's smile, Virid said, "Your confidence gratifies me, my golden one. But they might have more than swords and arrows to use against us. Remember, your lord keeps a wizard in his household."

"Do you truly think he has enough magic to threaten you? I've never seen him do more than make moving pictures in bonfires to amuse the children or conjure a sprinkle of rain during dry summers."

"I have dwelt here more than twice as long as you have been alive, long enough to sense hints of real power in the man. He may become a threat if the Baron feels sufficiently provoked." His tone turned grim. "And your heedless behavior might count as provocation."

She backed away from him and stood up. "So you're harping on that note again? Are you saying I should spend the rest of my life a prisoner in this cave, on the chance that if I show myself outside, I might fall into some phantom danger?"

"If you cannot exercise good judgment and listen to my warnings," he growled, "I may command you to do exactly that."

"Stay trapped here while you rant at me? I believe I would rather get eaten than listen to your scolding." Now that she felt sure he wouldn't harm her no matter how angry he became, his rebuke annoyed more than alarmed her.

"You deserve more than scolding, woman. You entered a settled region in broad daylight and frightened a man out of his wits. And not just any man, but one who has some wealth and influence in the village, whose tale will be heard with respect, is that not so?"

She reluctantly nodded.

"What would a human male do if his mate disobeyed a grave command that way? More than scold, I wager. He would probably beat her."

Folding her arms across her breasts, she matched his scowl with a defiant glare. "Are you going to beat me? That tail of yours would make a fine whip."

His frown turned to a sardonic smile. "Perhaps I should, but I have no desire to mar your soft skin. Nor do I want to squander energy in another change, after that strenuous flight. You say you would rather be eaten?" He bared his teeth like a wolf stalking a lamb. "Then I suppose I had better feast on you."

He leaped up and caught her in his arms. She made a token struggle, still irritated by his tyrannical commands. "Hush, my treasure, my pet. I do not wish to rob you of your freedom. I am only trying to protect you."

"I'm not a pet. Not sure I want to be a treasure, either."

"But you are." He ran his fingers through her hair. "Spun gold." When he massaged her scalp, she couldn't help sighing, feeling her resistance melt away. "Coral." His tongue circled the outline of her ear. She shivered, caught off guard by the sensation. "Rubies." He tweaked the firm tips of her nipples.

"What's coral?" Short of breath, she gasped out the question.

"A hard, pink substance, the shells of tiny sea animals. And you also have a pearl in your hidden grotto." He fingered her moist curls and the slick "pearl" in the midst of them.

Rowena shuddered. "Please—" Like a cat, she rubbed her head against his arm. His spicy scent prickled her nose.

"Or would you prefer the treasures that grow in nature? Such as ripe cherries." He nipped the side of her mouth. She involuntarily parted her lips for the entry of his tongue. He didn't linger there, though. "The apples of paradise." Lifting her breasts in his palms, he kissed each nipple in turn. He stroked her sides. "Skin white and smooth like lilies."

In turn, she ran her hand over his chest. His olive skin with its tiny scales looked like burnished metal, perhaps copper with a patina of age. He leaned into her caress, his throat vibrating with a sound almost like a purr.

One of his hands traveled down to her bottom, while the other explored the folds of her quim. "Rose petals with a folded bud and honey at the center." To her delighted surprise, he sank to his knees and tasted the wetness that pooled in her slit.

Trembling, she grasped his shoulders to keep from falling over. Steadying herself, she smoothed the silver-blue crest of his hair with one hand. It felt softer than she'd expected. "You're only trying to beguile me with all this dalliance—and fanciful words."

"Have you never heard such language before?" He hummed into her tender flesh, setting up vibrations that made her head spin.

She giggled. She had trouble shaping an answer with the distraction of the tickle in her clitoris. "Only in ballads. Great lords and ladies make love like that, so I've heard. Our village lads talk only of swiving ."

He looked up at her. His green eyes glowed. "And fucking?"

She suspected he used that word purely to watch her blush. "Just when they think the girls aren't listening."

"I would rather do it than speak of it. But first, I promised to eat you. Spread your legs for the feast." By the last words, his voice turned hoarse, with a hint of a growl. The hungry glint in his eyes made her heart race.

Still holding onto him, she planted her feet apart. Raising his head, he licked her navel. The unexpected touch made her flinch. He clasped her hips more firmly and traced a wet trail down her stomach and back up again. With a sigh, she yielded to his feasting as the point of his tongue mapped her lower abdomen. It skimmed along the top of the triangle of hair. She gasped when he nuzzled her curls. Now, she thought, he would soothe the part that ached for him. Instead, he skipped to her legs. He planted a kiss behind each knee, then nipped an upward path, his hot breath searing her thighs. He lapped the creases of each one in turn, avoiding the inner folds that yearned for his tongue. She threw her head back and arched her spine.

After several minutes of spiraling gradually closer to her center he probed inside her and licked up and down while her hips undulated. He seemed to sense the moment when she started to throb with an intolerable tingle in her bud. His tongue found and eased that tingle. Her legs quivering, she clutched his shoulders harder. The tip of his tongue circled her clitoris over and over, never quite touching the peak, where she needed it most. She felt tight enough to burst. When she groaned with the urgency of her need, he flicked the spot that yearned for relief. Faster and faster he lapped, strumming the peak hardest just as she tumbled over the precipice into the abyss of her release.

When she emerged from the moment of oblivion, he stood up, embracing her with his cock pulsing against her abdomen. "Now you," she panted, clasping his hardness. She wanted to inflict on him the same desperate craving he'd made her feel.

For a minute he thrust into her palm, his eyes half-closed in pleasure, but then he pulled back. "Not this way." Taking her hand, he drew her to the portal and shimmered into dragon form.

Still melting from her fulfillment, she easily flowed into the same shape. "You said you were too tired to change again."

"Ah, but feasting on you has restored my strength." He took flight. She followed him to a nearby meadow on a hillside. When she landed, he swooped down upon her. Before she realized what was happening, he straddled her body. "I want you hard and fast this time." The fierce snarl in his voice ignited her desire all over again. His fangs clamped onto her neck, not deep enough to hurt through the armor of her scales. The sting of his bite shot bolts of lightning through her. She felt his pole against her flanks.

Burning for him, she lashed her tail sideways and spread her rear legs. His cock drove into her. She bucked under him, her claws raking the ground. While he pounded in and out, they shredded the turf with their talons. Another climax shuddered over her. Fire shot from her mouth, and his fire merged with it. Roaring, she twisted her neck around to bite his shoulder.

The flavor of his blood inflamed her further. She wrenched free of him and rolled onto her back. He loomed over her, his scarlet cock jutting out. He plunged inside again. With all four feet, she dug her claws into his sides. Clutching each other with their talons, they tumbled over and over, roaring in their frenzy. Her head reeling, she convulsed with the force of his thrusts.

Finally, they lay still on the churned-up ground. She breathed out a fiery sigh of contentment. *I could never have known this ecstasy in my human life!*

Chapter Five

🙟

Three nights later Rowena woke to find the silk she lay on damp with perspiration. She sat up, wondering what had disturbed her. A silver chime echoed in her head, as if a bell had ceased ringing the instant before she had awakened. A chime in a dream, perhaps, though she couldn't remember what she had dreamed. The night air chilled the moisture on her skin. As always, she slept naked and human. In the perpetual pearly glow that emanated from the cave walls, she glanced at the treasure heap, where Virid slept in dragon shape. In sleep they always reverted to their respective natural forms, as they did whenever they needed to recover from over-exertion. Maintaining a dragon body took effort for her, and it appeared that even for an old, powerful creature such as Virid, remaining human for too long could be a strain. He showed no sign of waking at her movement. Since her disastrous adventure, he trusted her not to fly away on her own. Wrapping herself in a shawl, she walked to the entrance and surveyed the dark landscape by the light of the full moon.

A strange sensation stirred in the pit of her stomach. Not nausea, certainly not lust, though the flutter of excitement had some kinship with lust. A shiver coursed through her. She stretched out her bare arms, and the moonlight seemed to flow over them like water. She moaned aloud.

Behind her coins jingled as the dragon shifted on his bed of treasure. Rowena turned to see his eyes glittering in the depths of the cave. His voice rumbled, "Are you ill?"

"No, of course not. That is, I don't think so." She took a few steps back inside. "I feel odd. But it is surely nothing important."

"We cannot be certain of that." He unfolded his sinuous length from the treasure and walked to her. "Odd in what way?"

She described her sensations. With a flare of his nostrils, he inhaled the dampness between her breasts. She sighed and leaned on his arched neck. He led her to the sleeping alcove and curled around her, his tail resting across her legs. His tongue flickered over her stomach, making her leg muscles tighten with a tingle of pleasure.

"Is it possible—?" He covered her midriff with his splayed claws. "Yesss."

"What is it?" She squirmed, rubbing her back against the smooth scales of his chest.

Heat from his touch seeped into her skin and spread through her. "Behold," he said. A pale, green glow radiated from her abdomen.

She stared in wonder at the aura outlining the lower part of her body. "What's happening?"

"My magic confirms what I suspected from your scent and flavor. I hardly dared hope for it so soon." His tongue-tip kissed each of her nipples in turn. "You are bearing my child."

Her heart hammered as she watched the enchanted light fade away. "Are you sure? Virid, I don't know whether I am ready to become a mother. I'm afraid."

"Of what? I will not allow anything to harm you." He clasped her tighter against his chest. His breathing and the ponderous drumbeat of his heart filled her ears.

"I'm not frightened about things that might attack from outside. It's carrying a dragon babe that scares me."

She feared that admission might anger him, but he just calmly asked, "Why? You do not view my seed as a curse, the way your ignorant neighbors would, do you?"

Rowena shook her head. "How can I carry a young dragon, a wyrmling, in my womb? Suppose it grows too large?" A terrible image she had not thought of until that moment leaped into her mind. "What if it rips me apart with fangs and claws?"

"That will not happen. Remember, your grandam safely bore a dragon's offspring."

"But my mother's half human, and she has never looked or acted like anything but human. I'm part dragon, so our baby will be more than half dragon. Perhaps it won't be safe for me."

"Yes, you *are* part dragon. Therefore you have no need for concern."

She turned sideways to snuggle closer to him. How strange to find comfort in a giant reptile's embrace. "How long until I give birth? Nine months, like an ordinary woman?"

"I do not know. Perhaps you will follow the human pattern, perhaps a dragon's, or some time span in between. She-dragons do not give birth to live young. They remain gravid for two months, then lay a single egg, which they must keep warm until it hatches."

She leaned back to stare up at him. "Are you saying I might have to brood an egg like a hen?"

"We can only wait. Matings like ours are so rare no one could predict the outcome."

Trembling, she pulled the shawl tightly around her shoulders. "You're overjoyed at this, aren't you?"

"I want you to rejoice, too. And you will, once you become accustomed to the idea." His claws gently combed through her unbound hair. "Forget your fears. Sleep."

Next morning she woke before her mate and touched her bare stomach in wonder. Had she really seen a luminous halo there last night? Yes, she had to accept that it had actually happened. She had gotten with child by a dragon.

Virid, sprawled on the treasure heap, stretched, blew a puff of smoke, and opened his eyes. "My jewel." He melted into human form, reclining on his side with his head supported on one hand. Even in man shape, his eyes glittered when they fixed on her.

Rowena blushed under his steady gaze. She scanned his body and watched his cock rise from its nest of silvery hair as if her stare woke it to life. Her quim grew wet, ready to welcome it. However strange and even frightening their union might be in some ways, she couldn't deny the thrill his carnal pleasuring gave her. She held out her arms.

He hurried to her, lay beside her on the cushions, and gathered her into an embrace. She ran her hands up and down his arms, enjoying the silken sheen of his skin. It gleamed in the constant, soft glow emanating from the cave walls. His mouth covered her parted lips. Her tongue eagerly met the tip of his. Licking the inside of her lips, he nibbled his way from one corner of her mouth to the other. One of his hands alighted on her waist and traveled up to her breasts. Her nipples tightened. Still dueling with her tongue, he brushed his palm over one peak. With a sigh, she draped one leg over his and snuggled closer to bring the tip of his cock into contact with her quim.

To her dismay, he broke off the kiss and removed his hand from her breast. "Don't stop," she murmured, trying to force his fingers back to her taut nipple.

"I must." He shifted his hips away from hers and kissed her lightly on the forehead.

She tweaked one of his nipples, delighted with the way it hardened instantly like her own. "You don't want to fuck me anymore?" The word still felt strange in her mouth, but she spoke it sometimes because it seemed to fuel his ardor.

"Of course I do. I will never cease to want that. But we cannot take any chances of harming the infant. As I explained, our mating is unique, so nothing is certain." He smoothed her hair and fingered the nape of her neck.

"I see." She sat up and folded her arms with a half-serious pout. "To you I'm nothing but a brood mare. Now that I'm breeding, you lose all interest in me."

"Woman, you know very well that is nonsense," he growled.

"How do I know?"

He glanced down at his erect cock. It lengthened while she stared at it with him, and the thick head turned dark crimson. "You can see my interest with your own eyes. And feel it." He guided her hand to his shaft. It felt like a burning brand in her palm.

"But you're not interested enough to put it inside me." She couldn't suppress a sly smile at her own teasing.

"There are other ways to find satisfaction." He closed his fist around her hand and pumped up and down. Sighing with pleasure at his excitement, she followed his lead. He released her hand, leaving her to set the pace. Long, slow strokes made him heavy-lidded with desire, his face flushed. Her thumb skimmed the ridge around the head of his penis, wringing stifled moans from him. She jiggled his balls in her fingers, while he caressed the back of her neck and brushed each of her nipples so lightly she could scarcely keep from begging for firmer pressure. His cock expanded and grew still harder in her clasp. With a groan, he squeezed her hand. "Stop!"

"Why?" She tightened and released her grip, reveling in the way he panted with need.

"I want your mouth." He tangled his fingers in her hair. She gasped. "Suckle me!"

Made bold by his urgent tone, she nipped his neck, then kissed her way down his body, flicking her tongue every inch of the way. When she reached his nipples, hard as pebbles, he held himself rigidly motionless while she lapped them. Only his harsh breathing betrayed her effect on him. Once she started farther down, he broke his stillness to shift impatiently under her slow progress. She swirled her tongue in his navel, the way he'd once done to her, and savored his hiss of surprise. His hips pumped, and he pressed on her shoulders to guide her. When her lips finally touched the head of his cock, he groaned aloud.

She gave the swollen knob a tentative lick. He eased between her lips, his muscles quivering as if he could scarcely keep from thrusting inside. She circled the head with her tongue.

"Yessss." His fingers massaged her hair. "More!"

Anchoring herself by gripping his thighs, she lapped up and down the shaft. It leapt under her tongue. When she skimmed the tip, she tasted a drop of salty fluid. She opened her mouth and rubbed the head of his cock around the inside of her lips. The contrast between the silky surface and the stiff flesh thrilled her. When she sucked it in and out between her pursed lips, the flesh between her thighs twitched with eagerness to feel that same motion. Her clitoris thickened so that she had to cross her legs to relieve the ache.

Remembering how he'd tormented her with his tongue, she licked faster, spiraling around his shaft and teasing the opening at the tip. He stiffened harder than she had ever felt him before. Pressing a finger into the ridge behind his balls, she felt a throbbing deep within.

"Now!" he cried. "I have to spend!" With his hand on the back of her head, he flexed his hips to plunge deeply into her mouth. Her tongue circled the end of his cock while he thrust in and out. She sealed her lips around him to suckle until she felt his whole body turn rigid. His cock pulsed, and hot fluid shot into her mouth. Clutching his buttocks, she swallowed his seed and held him in her mouth until he went limp with satisfaction.

Her sheath throbbed with longing to receive his hardness. But he had refused to penetrate her. She wiggled up the length of his body, and he wrapped her in a tight embrace. "Help me," she gasped. "I need—"

He reached between her legs. His caress on her bud drew a moan from her. "Is this what you need?"

"Oh, yes! Inside me!"

He nuzzled her hair. "Inside you? Where?" She heard the smile in his voice.

"In my—my cunt." A hot flush flooded her face and breasts.

Instantly, he plunged his fingers into her. She arched her back and rocked in time with the exquisite motion. He found a spot that burned with almost painful intensity when he rubbed it. Piercing sweetness suffused her whole body. She closed her eyes to immerse herself in it.

"No," he whispered. "Look at me."

She obeyed, staring into the smoldering, green fire of his eyes. Her head spun with dizziness. She felt she might fall off the edge of the earth if she let go of him.

"I have never seen eyes so blue as yours," he murmured. "Like the sky. I could fall into them and drown." He quickened the dancing of his fingers. "Let me drown while you soar to the heights."

By now she could hardly understand his words. She rocked faster, his face a blur before her half-open eyes. Between the pressure and stroking inside her and the merciless strumming of her clitoris, she was melting, shattering—

She collapsed in his arms, with the flavor of him still on her lips, and trembled with pleasure at the warmth of his breath rustling her hair. His skin, like hers, felt slick with sweat. She kissed his cheek, tasting salt.

"You see," he murmured, "we need not sacrifice any of the delights we have shared. I shall always desire you, and I rejoice that you desire me."

"Yes, I do." She couldn't deny that feeling. But did she also want the child she carried? She still had deep-rooted doubts about that.

Over the next few weeks, Rowena suffered none of the aches and nausea she had seen her mother endure in pregnancy. She didn't even find herself drowsier than usual, only ravenously hungry. The dragon caught wild game for her every day. Tired of spending so many monotonous hours in the cave, she began hunting with him more often. In dragon form, she had no qualms about devouring a rabbit or deer raw, still steaming with life as its blood soaked into the earth. Sometimes Virid showed her where wild berries grew or guided her by night to an orchard temporarily left unguarded, to let her fill a basket with fruit while he kept watch. Human beings, he said, could not remain healthy on meat alone. She had shed the last of her misgivings about eating uncooked fruit, considering how quickly she had accepted a diet of freshly killed flesh.

He encouraged her to fly with him but snarled in protest when she ventured out on her own. "After your narrow escape at the mill, I cannot feel easy about having you wander the countryside alone," he admonished one day when he caught up with her on a peak where she could scan the horizon and see the Baron's keep on a distant hilltop and the villages and hamlets that owed homage to him scattered across the landscape like wooden blocks.

She stretched her wings with an impatient flap. "You speak as if I'm a child or a pet. I'm a grown woman and the mother of your babe, as you won't let me forget."

"Grown in human years, but very young as a dragon."

She snorted smoke from her nostrils. "How long do dragons live?"

"A thousand years or more. I have never seen one of my kind die of old age. When ancient dragons become weary of life, they take refuge in remote, well-hidden lairs. Whether they die or merely sleep, no one knows for certain."

His casual mention of a thousand-year lifespan chilled Rowena. Hiding that reaction, she asked, "Will I live that long?"

Viridiseffulgentissimus gave her a long, unblinking stare. "Again, I know not. With your dragon blood awakened you have a chance at centuries of life."

"It's possible, then?" At his slow nod, she said, "So when I'm a hundred years old do you still plan to watch me like a bird with a single fledgling?"

He tossed his head like a horse. "You have many years to go until you reach your first hundred."

"Well, if you keep me like a hooded falcon, I won't know how to survive even then, will I?"

"If you are truly eager to learn dragon ways," he said, "you should spend more time in this shape. Except while hunting, you insist on remaining human hour after hour."

"But I am human. Human first."

"If you continue to think that way," he said, "you will remain weak, and you will put yourself in danger."

Confused, she sprang into the sky, where the rush of wind could blow away the sadness that clouded her mind. Viridiseffulgentissimus followed, overshadowing her with his wings as usual. Now that the freshness of the experience had worn off, she felt that the adventure of becoming a dragon did not live up to its promise, not when her mate kept her tethered so closely. Besides, she couldn't shake her worries about her family. Little Harold had obviously been sick when she'd seen him. Had he recovered or died? Constantly watched, how could she find out?

A plan occurred to her, a simple way to make contact with her people. The first step required that she learn to read and write, something Virid himself had suggested. Back at the cave, she broached the subject. "I have nothing to do all day. I'm used to hard work, and there's none here. No cooking or baking. Almost no cleaning." She had made a crude broom out of twigs to sweep the cavern's floor every day and brush the worst of the cobwebs from the chests, casks, and loose heaps of treasure that made up the dragon's hoard. That task took little time. "No animals to tend. Not even any laundry to speak of. At home, we spent a full day each week on that." She washed her undertunics and hose in the bathing pool when necessary, but where outer clothing was concerned, the hoard included such an abundance of gowns and kirtles that she never needed to wear any garment more than once if she chose not to. "Until the baby comes, I'll sit idle most of the time."

Virid, sitting on a closed chest in human form, scanned her with a puzzled expression. "You miss all that drudgery? You should be glad of freedom from it."

"In a way, I am. But not without something to take its place." She flipped open one of the boxes and took out a small, leather-bound volume. "Teach me to read, the way you said you would."

"Very well. But you cannot begin with a book like that. We shall need writing materials." He rummaged around in a smaller box for a sheet of blank parchment, a handful of quills, and a vial of black powder. Leading Rowena to sit on a box, using a larger chest for a table, he showed her how to mix the powder with water to make ink. "You say you know your letters?"

"Mostly, or I did once. I might have forgotten some." Clutching a quill in her right hand, she tried to imitate the way Virid held his.

"Then let us begin at the beginning. This is A." He dipped the quill pen and marked the letter on the parchment.

"Of course I know that one. It's the end of my name." It had been a long time, though, since Grandmother had made her practice writing. She found the process awkward, and her A looked crude next to Virid's.

"Do not concern yourself with elegance yet," he said. "Concentrate on remembering the shape."

After an hour of drill, the alphabet and its sounds came back to Rowena. That basic knowledge was a long way from mastery of the skill, though. She ran her fingers over the binding of the book she had set aside. "When do you think I'll be able to read something like this?"

"You have a great deal to learn before that," he said. "Most of these books are written in Latin or Greek, of which you know nothing. I must first teach you to read your own Saxon tongue."

Since that was exactly what Rowena wanted, she made no objection. "Can you tell me what's in the books, though? What about this one?"

Picking up the small volume, he said, "This is the *Metamorphoses* of Ovid, a poet of Rome's golden age. Shall I read to you from it?"

She nodded. Her right hand felt so cramped from the unfamiliar task that she knew she had to rest it before she tried again.

Cuddled up with Virid on the sleeping cushions, she listened to his translation from a section of the long poem, tales of pagan gods pursuing shy maidens who changed into flowers or trees to escape their suitors. "Do you think such things really happened?" she asked when he closed the book to save more for another time.

He wound a lock of her hair around his fingers. "I cannot say for certain, but I doubt it."

"We change from dragon to human and back, though. And I've heard of men who take the shape of wolves."

"That is different from a woman transforming into a tree. That would be far beyond the power of dragon magic, much less that of a merely human sorcerer like your Baron's wizard. It would take the enchantment of a deity."

"You don't think the heathen gods really existed, then?"

He reclined on the cushions and drew her closer to his side. "I have never met one, nor have I heard of any other dragon who has."

Tracing swirls with her fingertip on his gleaming, olive-skinned chest, she said, "I've heard the old gods were really demons in disguise."

"Do you believe that?" His open palm stroked down her side to her flank, then strayed to her arse. They were both naked. Virid never wore clothes, and Rowena hadn't bothered to dress when resuming human form after their flight. Though she sometimes enjoyed trying on the silken robes and fur-lined cape, her awakened dragon blood kept her warm enough in the lair with no covering.

"I don't know. It's said dragons are a kind of demon, too. Tales claim the Devil sometimes appears as a dragon."

He emitted a contemptuous growl. "Typical human folly. I am certainly no demon, nor any of my kin."

She rubbed her head, catlike, against his shoulder. "I know that now. If you were a demon, I'd have to be one, too, because I'm part dragon. But I do wonder if dragons have souls. Do you?"

His brows arched in obvious surprise at the question. "How would I know? I have no idea whether souls even exist."

She stared at him in shock. She had never heard anyone suggest that possibility before. "If dragons don't have souls, do I?"

"So now you are becoming a philosopher, my golden one?" A laugh rumbled deep in his chest. "Do not trouble yourself about such things. Enjoy what your new life gives you. Such as this." He bent to kiss her.

Whenever she expressed worries of any kind, more often than not he tried to distract her with dalliance. To her annoyance, she usually succumbed to those distractions. She turned her face away, ignoring the frisson she felt when his tongue brushed her lips, and said, "I was brought up to worry about those things. I can't just stop thinking about them, any more than I can stop missing my family and friends."

He frowned. "That complaint again? Dragons do not need company, except perhaps that of a mate."

"Well, I'm not all dragon. My human half still has its needs."

"Needs that you will be happier if you overcome." He stood up and reached for her hand. "Shed your human form and fly with me. I want to share a new pleasure with you."

"Again so soon? What do you want to show me, another kind of lovemaking?"

"Not this time. I have an adventure to offer you." He strode toward the exit.

Curious despite herself, she followed. On the ledge, they both transformed, and she launched herself aloft with him.

Following in his wake, she flew higher and farther than ever before. Above the clouds, the sun blazed in her eyes, yet the clear air blew chill across her wings and whistled through her bared teeth. The landscape spread out beneath them as, she thought, the eyes of God Himself must see it.

Her wings began to ache by the time her mate spiraled toward the earth on a plateau wedged between two hills. Flower-strewn grass surrounded a blue lake. Viridiseffulgentissimus folded his wings and waited for her to glide to a landing beside him. "See that rivulet trickling downhill?" He swiveled his neck to indicate the narrow, rapid stream. "That is the origin of the river that waters your village."

"We're so high," she marveled. "I'd wager not even the Baron has ventured this far. Then, why would he care to?" Laughter rippled from her in a burst of flame. "There's nothing here to profit him or add to his prowess in battle." She savored the scent of the crisp air. "If I'd never come to you, I wouldn't have seen this place, either. I never imagined traveling so far from home."

"This is only the beginning. You told me you used to crave adventure? When our child has grown old enough, perhaps I will take you to the shores of Greece, the mountains of Carpathia, the sands of Egypt, or even far Cathay where they spin the silk that drapes so beautifully on your delicate body."

She laughed again at the extravagant compliment, as well as at the idea of traveling to such exotic lands, which sounded as likely a destination as the Garden of Eden. He stretched his neck over hers and nuzzled her. The friction of his scales against hers made her quiver with delight. She whirled around and gave him a playful nip.

Leaping backward, he spread and flapped his wings, raising a wind. "Now, join me in the lake."

He folded his wings tightly to his sides and dove into the water. A waterspout splashed high into the air when he plunged beneath the surface. She dubiously eyed the deep tarn. It must be deep if a full-grown dragon could dive into it. She didn't want to behave like a coward in her mate's presence, though. She leaped in an arc and dived after him.

Instinct made her draw a long breath before jumping. Her nostrils automatically compressed to shut out the water. She squeezed her eyes closed against the impact. Icy liquid enveloped her. Forcing herself to open her eyes, she saw schools of fish scattering out of her way and the huge body of the dragon gliding gracefully beside her, with his wings spread as if flying. She imitated him and thrilled to the silken flow of the water over her wing membranes. Venturing a glance down, she saw the lake bottom shimmering far below.

Over his shoulder, Viridiseffulgentissimus threw a challenging look at her. With a brisk flap of his wings and tail, he shot ahead. She picked up speed to swim after him. He sped through the water like a falcon through the air. He hurtled into the midst of a shoal of fish. A snap of his jaws caught one of them. Eager to match his skill, she gnashed her teeth amid the roiling mass of frightened creatures. Just before the pressure in her lungs increased almost to pain, she captured one large fish. Her mate shot up to the surface, and she followed him. Cold water splashed around her and flowed down her sides, glittering like countless tiny crystals in the blinding sun.

She swam to shore, blinking until her eyes adjusted to full daylight again. She gulped down her fish, salty and refreshingly cool, while Viridiseffulgentissimus ate his own catch. The water sparkled on his scales like rainbow-hued gems. Her breath caught in her throat at his beauty.

"Now we dive still deeper." He hurtled himself into the lake again.

Filling her chest with air, she dove in his wake. Underwater she saw the iridescent streak of his body swimming almost straight down. Within minutes, they glided within a dragon-height's span of the lake bottom. The current of their passage stirred patches of weeds in which tiny fish darted. Her mate led her to a heap of white sticks that at first glance she took for the wreckage of a boat. But who would sail across this mountain tarn so far from any suitable site for a town?

With a closer look, she made out the shape of an elongated, fanged skull. The "sticks" were gigantic bones. A creature twice the size of a dragon had died here long ago. Around the neck of the skeleton was looped a silver chain with a pale, oval gem hanging from it. Viridiseffulgentissimus snagged it with a claw and surged toward the surface.

When they emerged onto the bank, she asked, "What kind of bones are those?"

"Why, those of a lake dragon, of course. Centuries ago many of them lived in the waters of this land. A few still dwell in the deep lochs of the highlands beyond the Roman wall." He held out the necklace to her. Now she could distinguish the color of the stone, sky-blue with swirls of rose in its depths. "This is a moonstone," he said. "For you, my treasure." He hung the chain around her neck.

"Is it magic?"

"Not as you understand the word, but it is rare and beautiful, and therefore you should have it."

Touching the moonstone with a claw-tip, she marveled at the glow of the colors at its center. "I have never seen anything so wonderful."

His tongue flicked her ear. "Change," he said.

She flowed into human shape. The cool breeze on her naked skin momentarily made her shiver, but her mate's body, like a living oven, quickly warmed her. The chain dangled loosely, with the moonstone hanging below her breasts. Virid's tongue looped around her neck and teased the hollow of her throat. Trembling, she leaned against his side. He swept her hair over her shoulder to lick the nape of her neck. Chills raced down her spine, and he followed them with rapid flickers of his tongue.

"How can you doubt that I cherish you and consider you beautiful?"

"Show me," she murmured.

He delicately sifted her unbound hair through his claws. His tongue circled her neck again and explored the hollow of her throat and the valley between her breasts. Her nipples puckered, and her breath became quick and shallow. She stared into the glow of his green eyes, feeling entranced like a mouse under the gaze of a serpent. Yet he looked at her with a hunger quite different from a snake's for its prey, as if the sight of her enraptured him and cast him, too, into a trance. How far they had come since her terror in the first moment she'd seen him.

One of his claws traced a tingling line down the center of her chest, while he tasted each nipple in turn. Impatient, she wanted to embrace him and pull him down to her, but her arms barely reached around his neck, and her merely human strength had no hope of overcoming his resistance. She had to squirm helplessly while his tongue spiraled around each breast and worked its way over her stomach to the damp curls at its base.

She slid to the ground and lay on her back, legs spread in invitation. The tip of his tongue probed her cleft. Letting out a hissing breath, she arched her hips. He licked up and down the moist folds, and with every stroke, she melted still more. Her clitoris tightened to an unbearable ache. She could tell by the way his tongue fleetingly brushed there that he knew what she yearned for. She couldn't force out the words to beg for it, only moan and clutch at him.

When she felt about to shatter with need, he settled into a steady licking of her swollen bud. He curled his tail around her and inserted the end of it into her sheath. His tongue strummed her harder, faster. She felt herself plummeting toward the cliff-edge of release—a scream ripped from her throat—she plunged into the abyss—

Heavy-lidded, she gazed into his eyes, close to hers with his huge head resting beside her. "You've had no satisfaction," she said when she could breathe again.

"That matters not. Your pleasure fulfills me."

Her eyes prickled with moisture. No lad of her village would ever have spoken thus. She folded her hand around the smooth hardness of the moonstone. "You were right," she said, rolling face down on the grass. "This is a new kind of adventure."

"And, as I said, only the beginning of many greater ones."

Chapter Six

ജ

Over the next fortnight, she relearned the sounds of the alphabet and began to read. Virid's hoard held almost no books in her native language. He explained to her that whenever people wrote anything of importance, they used Latin. Records were usually kept in French. He managed to unearth a few writings in the Saxon vernacular for her to practice with, such things as merchants' inventories and lists of village births and deaths. She didn't object to the dull, everyday subject matter, for it contained many of the words she would need for the message she planned to send. Whenever she was not exercising her wings and hunting, she spent most of her waking hours studying and prodding Virid to teach her faster.

"Why this obsession with letters and words?" he asked her one evening as she sat by the cave entrance taking advantage of the fading sunlight. "Put away your parchment and fly with me."

Rowena shrugged off his touch on her shoulder. "Later, after the moon rises. I don't want to waste what's left of the day."

He responded with a wordless hiss of annoyance.

"You told me dragons value wisdom. Don't you want me to learn?"

"Of course, but you need not learn all the wisdom of the world in one day, or even one week."

"No fear of that." She impatiently brushed her hair back from her forehead. She couldn't admit her real motive for cramming every possible hour with study. He certainly would not approve of her writing to her family. But she had to find out whether her little brother had fallen victim to the typhoid fever raging through the village. "What else am I supposed to do with my time? I can't stand day after day of idleness."

With his glittering eyes fixed on her, he said, "Have you truly been so discontented?"

"Not exactly discontented, but this life still feels strange to me. I have trouble resting with the same light coming from the walls every hour of the day and night. I'm tired of living on meat and fruit. I miss the other food I used to eat. I crave a loaf of bread with honey or a wedge of cheese. I even miss pease porridge. And, yes, sometimes I miss what you called the drudgery of ordinary work." The words tumbled out, even surprising herself. "And ale. I haven't had a mug of ale since you brought me here."

"Do you not prefer wine and mead?"

They often shared a few goblets of wine in the evenings, and she had developed a taste for the vintages of Burgundy. "I like them well enough, but that doesn't stop me from craving more ordinary fare sometimes."

"You miss your human life," he said in a deadly quiet tone.

"What did you expect? You stole me away from my family and friends."

"Friends? They scorned your ancestry and delivered you up for sacrifice."

Scrambling to her feet with the parchment and quill clutched in one hand, she glared at him. "True enough, I didn't have many friends, and they turned out to be false or too afraid to speak up. But at least I had girls my own age to talk with and my parents and brothers to care for me." Would she actually return to that world if she could? Perhaps not, given the treatment she'd received from the neighbors she had known all her life. Yet she resented having the choice snatched from her.

"I care for you. Do you not believe that yet?"

Rowena shoved past him into the cave and busied herself with putting the writing supplies away. "I believe you do in your own way. You care for me as your mate and the mother of your young." She touched her belly, more rounded than it had been a month earlier. "But it's not the same." She looked over her shoulder to find him hovering behind her. "Of course, I enjoyed our swiving, and I love taking dragon shape and flying with the wind. But I love my family, too."

"If you would cast away these human anxieties and regrets," he said, "you would attain happiness and freedom. You need to remain in woman shape only while you sleep, not the rest of the time. Embrace your dragon nature."

"And attain freedom?" She turned on him, with her hands on her hips. "I haven't noticed you giving me any of that yet. When I do take dragon form, you shadow every move I make. You want me to forget my family and my human life, yet you don't allow me a proper dragon life either."

"When you become strong enough to protect yourself—"

"Ballocks! That's only an excuse for not trusting me. You think if I got an occasional glimpse of home, I would leave you."

He flinched, as if the randomly flung accusation had struck the center of the target. "I simply desire your happiness, which you cannot have if you remain suspended between your two natures. Have you forgotten this?" Striding to the largest book chest, he pulled out the volume that contained the legend of St. George. He opened it to the gold-embossed picture of the knight standing over the prostrate dragon. "This is what human folk would do to you if they could. Forget their puny lives and choose your true self."

"You want me to live as a dragon, yet you want to keep me penned here at your pleasure! Would a true she-dragon accept this treatment?"

He bared his teeth, sharply pointed even in human form. "A full-blooded she-dragon would never want to fraternize with humankind."

"A she-dragon's mate would trust her out of his sight, instead of assuming she hadn't wit enough to be careful."

Virid gripped her shoulders, his fingers digging into her flesh. "Woman, you try my patience!" With a long, hissing breath, he relaxed his grasp. "What do you want of me? Be warned, I will not tolerate any trespassing on human lands."

Rowena's heartbeat quickened. She struggled to keep triumph from showing on her face. "Prove your faith in me. Allow me some of the freedom you mentioned."

"How?"

"Let me fly alone for part of each day. I vow not to let any human eyes see me without your permission."

He studied her face as if searching for any hint of deception. "You make this promise freely?"

She nodded. "If you meet my condition. If you keep watching me every minute, I can't promise what I might do."

"Very well." He sighed and ran his hands down her arms in a slow caress to clasp her hands. "I accept your vow. When do you plan to enjoy your freedom?"

"I think I'll start now." Freeing her hands from his, she stripped off her gown and underlinen. She wanted to test his compliance with the bargain. At the same time, her behavior would assure him that she would keep her word. She didn't intend to break the vow. Her plan didn't involve having anyone see her.

When she launched herself from the ledge, Virid stood there as a man, watching her. That behavior struck her as a good omen. By not changing into his dragon shape, he seemed to be reassuring her that he would not follow. Still, she would take no chances on her first couple of flights. She headed away from the inhabited region to fly over uncleared forest. Recalling her girlish daydream of living in the woods as an outlaw, like Maid Marian with Robin Hood, she wondered what it would be like to walk under those venerable trees. Perhaps on some other day she could find out.

The setting sun tinged the horizon with violet and rose. Soaring higher, Rowena watched the crimson orb sink behind the hills while the blue of the sky faded into twilight. She scented moisture in the cool upper air. When she circled back toward the east, she saw clouds gathering. By the time she reached the cave, raindrops were spattering her scales. She opened her mouth to catch the windswept rain.

Sighting her approach, Viridiseffulgentissimus leaped from the ledge, shifting shape in midair. He flew around her, then paced her, wingtip to wingtip. "You returned."

"Did you seriously think I might not?" She wasn't sure whether she felt offended by his doubt or flattered by the concern it indicated.

He hesitated for several wing beats before answering. "I am not certain what I thought. I am grateful for your return." Instead of landing at the cave entrance, he swooped down to a nearby hilltop. Rowena followed him. When she settled to the ground and folded her wings, he wrapped his around her. "Rowenaureadulcima. My treasure. I wish only to give you joy, delights you could never imagine in your former life. Like this." His serpentine tongue lapped raindrops from her neck. Shivering, she surrendered to the pleasure of his

150

caresses. He chased the rivulets over her body until he had licked her from neck to tail-tip.

By then her tail was twitching with restlessness that coursed through her veins and settled between her rear legs. She spread them wide, and he circled behind her. His sinuous tongue lashed her slit. In this body she had no clitoris to form the center of her need. Instead, all the aching tightness settled deep inside her. He inserted his tongue into her sheath and rubbed in time with her frantic humping.

"Change," he ordered.

She melted into her human shape, still shaking with hunger for him. The sensation of his tongue whipping in and out of her while her body compressed from dragon to woman made her scream in mingled shock and excitement. On hands and knees, her fingernails gouging the turf, she arched her back to beg for deeper penetration. One of his claws trailed down her spine. The fiery track of its point sharpened her craving still more. His tongue-tip found a burning spot far inside her sheath and stroked it in time with the rocking of her hips. Ecstasy radiated from that spot to flood her entire body.

Limp, panting, she allowed him to roll her onto her back. He still held his dragon shape. She saw his stallion-like cock jutting out.

He licked raindrops from her breasts. "When you have given birth, we can mate as dragons again. I yearn for that."

"Turn into a man so I can pleasure you." Sitting up, she reached under his abdomen to cup his penis, almost too big for her hand to fit around.

"No." He blew a puff of smoke that instantly turned to steam in the rain. "I want to spend in my true form." He lay down on his side, with his cock engorged to a deep red.

She skimmed her palm over the taut flesh. "How?" Her sheath rippled in anticipation, despite the impossibility of his entering her this way.

One of his forelegs curled around her to draw her close. She automatically opened her legs. The head of his penis settled between her thighs, its round tip resting on her clitoris.

"Move," he ordered.

Bracing her legs against him, she slid up and down his shaft. Slowly at first, she savored the glide of his rigid flesh on her tight bud. With each cycle of upward and downward motion, she quivered with eagerness, and a groan rumbled in his chest. His claws held and guided her, clasping just tightly enough to prick her skin without pain.

He urged her to a faster rhythm. She felt him swelling between her legs. The friction on her bud and between her folds of tender flesh sent the now-familiar waves of delight crashing over her. His body quaked with passion, and the scalding heat of his seed flooded her. The sensation drove her to the edge all over again.

When she convulsed in her final delirium, he coiled around her and held her with all four limbs until her shudders died away. Torrents of rain drenched their entwined bodies.

* * * * *

Over the next few days, Rowena flew with Virid whenever he invited her. She also regularly flew by herself an hour or two, varying the time of day or night and the length of her absence. She wanted to be sure the dragon accepted her unpredictable flights and believed she would always come back without getting into trouble. Aside from the furtherance of her plan, she found that she enjoyed soaring alone in the moonlight even more than her daylight forays.

On rocky hillsides she practiced another skill she would need. She picked up small stones, ascended high into the air, and dropped them one by one onto the ground, aiming for targets she had scratched in the turf. At first her stones missed more often than they hit. Soon, though, her keen dragon eyes enabled her to learn how to hit her mark.

Her thoughts hadn't advanced beyond the prospect of communicating with her grandmother. If Harold was deathly ill or some other disaster had happened at home, what could Rowena do about it? She simply felt she had to know. It did occur to her that if she asked Virid's permission to visit her family, and he refused again, she could leave him. Did she want that? A chill gripped her insides at the thought. For one thing, deserting her mate would force her to bring up a mostly-dragon infant by herself. Yet, if that decision did eventually face her, she wanted to be prepared.

At heart she knew she could never live with her family again. Could she make a home for herself, though? What about her idea of living in the deep woods? As a dragon, she wouldn't need shelter and would have no trouble obtaining food.

Although she had no serious plans to abandon Virid, she began to use part of her "free" hours exploring the forest. She quickly discovered the trees grew too densely for a winged monster to descend through their branches. Instead, she landed on the verge of the woods, changed shape, and walked in. After many weeks of not bothering with shoes, her feet did not suffer from walking bare-soled on the leaf-strewn loam. The towering trees cast such deep shade that it muted the late summer heat to moist coolness. Little underbrush grew beneath them, so nothing impeded her leisurely stroll. She marveled at their massive trunks, like the pillars of a giant's hall.

About half an hour into the forest, she came upon a fallen tree. Vines covered its gigantic remains. Kneeling down, she discovered a hollowed space under it, almost like a miniature cave. Maybe some animal had denned there for a while. She considered crawling inside to check the size of the hole, but thoughts of beetles and spiders restrained her. Still, it might make a good hiding place to store things out of the weather. If she ever did feel compelled to leave Virid, she might want to have a few supplies stowed away.

Brushing dirt from her hands and knees, she turned back toward the edge of the forest. By exploring the countryside on her own, she had discovered that her dragon nature gave her a faultless sense of direction. She had no doubt of her ability to find the dead tree again. Once clear of the woods, she resumed dragon shape and flew to the lair, where Viridiseffulgentissimus awaited, impatient for a shared hour of flight and frolic. Though he never said so, she got the impression that he felt uneasy about her solitary ventures, even if he trusted her to stay clear of human settlements. Apparently her partial independence troubled him. Well, let it. He had better learn she wouldn't be treated like a possession.

In the following days, she began to accumulate a stash of items she thought she might need if she had to leave. A well-fed dragon, she had learned, slept long and hard. Her partial humanity meant that she often found herself awake while Virid slumbered. Although she wouldn't risk sneaking out of the lair at such times, because of his probable reaction if he did wake up and find her gone, she decided searching the boxes was safe enough. Her rummaging around the cave's chambers never seemed to disturb him.

She set aside a dagger with its sheath and belt, all wrapped in oiled cloth. With several layers of water-resistant cloth, the wrapping could easily hold several other small objects. In a stroke of luck, she later found a pouch of the same material. Between the two packages, she gradually tucked away several changes of clothes, a few quills and a vial of powdered ink, and a handful of coins. For outer clothing she chose men's breeches and tunics of green and russet. If she had to live in the forest, she couldn't do it gowned like a court lady. She also filched shoes and hose, as well as linen cloths and two shawls, in case she did find herself caring for a baby alone in the wilderness. Little by little, she cached the supplies in a small, empty side alcove, too cramped for Virid's dragon body. Since he had not been using it for storage so far, he would have no reason to go near it, even in human form.

Watching him sleep or lying curled up with him after love-play, she mused over her own actions. He called her his mate. Most of the time, she thought of herself that way. Yet she realized she did not consider herself wedded to the dragon as irrevocably as he did. If she shared his belief in their union, she would not be making plans for a future break that might or might not ever come to pass.

When she reached the stage where she felt confident of writing a letter that her grandmother could read, she debated how to deliver it without arousing Virid's suspicions. She didn't feel safe in relying on the depth of his sleep. Nor could she venture out while he was away hunting. If she made up some excuse not to fly with him, he would suspect ulterior motives when he returned and found she had left on her own.

Their evening flagon of wine suggested a possible solution to that problem. Virid often allowed her to draw their drinks from one of the casks. It would be a simple matter to add a dash of poppy syrup to his goblet. Did the drug work on dragons? And how much would she need to deepen his sleep? She could only try a dose at random. If it didn't work, she would have lost nothing, because Virid would have no reason to guess what she'd done.

She seized the opportunity that very day at twilight, while Virid disposed of the gnawed bones of a sheep they had devoured. During his last rest period she'd hidden one of the bottles of poppy syrup under her sleeping cushions. Since he left the tidying and replacing of the bed silks to her, he would not be likely to notice the bottle. She hurried to the rock shelf where she had already set out two flagons of different design. After splashing a few drops of the drug into the cup she intended for Virid, she rushed to hide the bottle again. As she plumped the cushions back into place, she already heard his wings flapping at the portal.

By the time he slithered into the great hall, raindrops sliding off his scales, Rowena stood quietly with a cup in each hand. She hoped he couldn't hear the racing of her heart. "Let me draw some mead for you, and we'll drink by the fire." She nodded toward the fire pit where embers smoldered after the roasting of the sheep.

"Mead?" When he completed his shift to human form, he gave her a questioning stare. "You usually prefer wine."

"It's a wet evening. Mead seems best for this weather." She spoke with her back to him while she headed for the cask that held the honey beverage, afraid he would recognize deception on her face. In truth, she chose the sweet wine in hopes it would disguise any strange flavor. She filled his goblet, then her own, and carried them to the sleeping alcove where Virid reclined on the cushions.

She swirled the liquid in his flagon before handing it to him and taking a sip from hers. Over the rim of her cup, she watched him drink. Her anxious scrutiny detected no change in his expression when he tasted the mead.

"Why do you stare at me so intently, my love?"

"Do I?" A blush spread over her face and neck. How could she expect to get away with lying to him? "I never get tired of looking at you. You're beautiful." That statement, at least, was true. His emerald eyes and, in human shape, burnished olive skin with its delicate pattern of tiny scales still fascinated her. He was even more glorious, though in a grand and terrible way, as a dragon.

"Indeed? I cannot recall any other human female paying me that compliment," he said with a wide, sharp-toothed grin. "So are you, my treasure. Beautiful. Like gold and mother of pearl." He placed a fingertip in the hollow of her breasts just above the neckline of the silken shift she wore. After weeks of this cave-dwelling life, seldom exposed to sunlight except in dragon form, she had in fact noticed her skin losing its tan and becoming almost pale enough to be called "pearl."

She took a swallow of her mead. "Finish your drink. I don't want to become tipsy alone."

"Have you any special plans after you have intoxicated me? Not that I need anything but yourself to produce that effect." Cupping the back of her head, he nipped her earlobe, then nibbled his way along her jaw to her mouth. A gasp of anticipation parted her lips for him. His tongue traced their outline, making her breath come quick and shallow. He tasted like honey.

His mention of "plans" cut into her excitement with a tremor of fear. Could he suspect? A second later, she realized guilt had led her thoughts astray, and the only plan he had in mind was seduction.

"Drink up," she said, forcing a teasing lilt into her voice, "and you'll find out." She drained her cup, suppressing a grimace at the sticky sweetness.

Virid followed her example. He put down his empty flagon, twined his fingers in her hair, and returned to feasting on her mouth. With a sigh of relief that he'd noticed nothing suspicious, she wrapped her arms around his neck and yielded to the pleasure of his kiss.

After long minutes of head-spinning delight, Virid pulled away from her. His palm skimmed her nipples through the cloth, but with no urgency. "Shall we rest first and carry out your plan when we awaken refreshed?" His eyes were heavy-lidded, his voice deep and slow.

"That would suit me well," Rowena said, although the fire in the pit of her stomach made her almost wish he would delay sleep long enough to quench it.

"Good night, then." With a final, light kiss, he withdrew to the treasure heap, where he shifted to dragon form and stretched out with eyes shut.

Chapter Seven

ဘ

She watched him, almost holding her breath, until twin curlicues of smoke from his nostrils signaled the rhythm of sleep. Anxiety doused any trace of lust. When she was finally sure he wouldn't wake anytime soon, she got out her writing materials to pen the note to her grandmother. She knew only enough words to compose a simple message, but she needed nothing more. She wrote, "Grandmother: I am alive and well. Tell my parents if you think it safe. Are they well? Are my brothers well? Leave an answer under a rock by the tree of tribute, and I will get it. With love, Rowena."

She folded the paper and wrapped it in two layers, first of oiled wool, then of leather. Tying the package with a leather thong, she attached the bronze amulet to it. That talisman would prove to Grandmother that the note came from Rowena. She only hoped Virid would not notice the amulet's disappearance. He hadn't taken any notice of it since the night she had arrived, and over the weeks it had become buried under shifting layers of coins. Its absence shouldn't be obvious.

She stripped off her shift and gathered up the packet as well as her bundles of hidden supplies. As long as she had the chance to sneak out, she might as well combine errands.

The rain was ending when she leaped into the air with the packages clutched in her claws. She first headed for the deep forest. Again she had to change shape in order to fit under the trees. Even as a woman, she retained enough of her newfound draconic directional sense to retrace her path straight to the fallen tree. She wedged her oilcloth-wrapped bundles as far into the hole as she could. Since she had not packed any food that could attract animals, she felt sure the cache would remain safe until she needed it, if ever.

That left only her message to deliver. She hurried to the edge of the woods as fast as she could to shapeshift and launch herself into the sky. She drove herself to the swiftest possible flight, her wings aching, her chest tight with the struggle for breath. With no way of knowing how long the poppy dose would affect the dragon, she didn't want to take chances with delay.

The moon peeping from behind the clouds helped her find the river that guided her to the village. She hoped its glow, although strong enough for her dragon eyes, would be too faint to allow a wakeful man or woman to spot her. When she reached her destination, she saw the glimmer of candlelight in only a few windows. Most houses were shuttered and dark, as they should be at this hour. Dawn came early in summer, and farmers had no reason to postpone much-needed sleep, especially on a wet night.

Circling over her family's holding, she focused on her grandmother's one-room cottage. At sunrise the old woman would emerge from her door to plod across the yard to the shared livestock shed and milk the single nanny goat allotted to her. She couldn't miss seeing the message packet if it lay on her front walk. Rowena circled as low as she dared, concentrating on the technique she had practiced with pebbles and rocks. She hovered for a second, clasping the small package in her claws, and let it drop. It landed on the stone slab outside her grandmother's door.

With a hissing smoke-puff of relief, she shot upward and raced for the cave. Now she needed to get back before Virid noticed her absence. She could do no more until she'd allowed time for Grandmother to read and answer the note.

Glad the rain had stopped, so that no telltale wetness could betray her unauthorized journey, Rowena changed back into a woman the moment she landed on the ledge. When she emerged from the entry tunnel into the great hall, coins clinked with the dragon's movement. She froze, one hand on her chest, the other bracing her against the wall.

He raised his head, eyes glittering. "My jewel? Is something wrong?"

"No." Could his keen ears catch the hammering of her heart? "I had trouble sleeping, and I went to the portal to look at the moon."

"Come lie with me." He extended a foreleg to beckon her.

She crossed the chamber and reclined in the circle of his front legs. He laid one across her body, claw-tips grazing her breasts. "Why are you breathing so heavily?"

She could hardly confess her solitary flight now. With a hand on her belly, she said, "Sometimes I have trouble getting enough air when I'm lying down. It presses on my ribs." That excuse held some truth, for the pregnancy had expanded alarmingly within the past week or two.

Virid's talons lightly skimmed the visible bulge. "Our youngling will be strong and vigorous. He grows faster than a human infant."

"Or maybe she." With the relief of knowing her mate didn't suspect her secret errand, Rowena found herself overcome by weariness. She hid a yawn behind her hand. "I might have a girl, like my grandmother."

"Perhaps." He seemed unperturbed by the suggestion.

"What, your dragon magic can't tell?"

He said with a ripple of laughter, "I cannot even divine whether the child will appear dragon or human. Having

161

waited so long for my true mate, I can wait with patience for the birth."

She snuggled up to him with her head pillowed on his torso, knowing that she would feel stiff and sore from dozing on the treasure pile but wanting to encourage him to fall back to sleep quickly. The longer they conversed, the more likely she would become nervous again and let him catch her in a lie about her evening's activity.

Hardly able to stand the delay, yet afraid of using the poppy syrup again too soon, Rowena waited until the second night afterward to slip the drug into Virid's evening drink again. Since the first dose had clearly taken effect but hadn't lasted very long, she increased the amount by a couple of drops. As soon as he slept, she flew to the tree where she had been sacrificed.

Upon landing, she saw nothing that looked like a message. In the faint moonlight, though, even dragon eyes could miss such a small object. She searched the ground at the foot of the dead tree, still draped with the remains of the ropes that had bound her. Nothing. Inhaling and exhaling in rapid hisses of frustration, she widened her circuit and turned over every rock. No letter.

She silently commanded herself not to panic. Lack of a note didn't necessarily mean Grandmother had not read the letter. It could mean only that she hadn't found time to sneak out and deliver a reply. The tree was a long walk from the village, especially for an old woman. Rowena leaped from the earth, her wings flailing the night air. She would simply have to return in a night or two.

The next day, she couldn't hide her dismal mood from the dragon. She had no appetite for apples from the basket he had filled on his latest orchard-robbing expedition. She barely nibbled the rabbit he roasted for her when she refused to change shape and eat it raw. When he read to her from a

Latin scroll of the lives of saints and martyrs that usually enthralled her, she fretted and lost the thread of the tale.

"What troubles you today?" he finally asked. "You seem unlike yourself. Perhaps you need to fly in the clear air and exercise your wings."

"I don't feel like flying." She wrapped her arms around her knees and edged away from him.

His whip like tongue encircled her neck and insinuated itself into her bodice. "Then another kind of exercise might help you relax."

Her skin itched with irritation at the caress that normally made her tremble with excitement. "I don't want that now, either. Just leave me alone."

"Can you not tell me why?" The wistful rather than impatient tone of his voice made her feel almost guilty about keeping secrets from him.

Unable to confess her problems in communicating with her family, she gave him a partial truth. "I've already explained what's bothering me. My body feels wrong, I'm worried about the baby, and I miss having my mother and grandmother to talk to, which you won't hear of. So why discuss it at all?"

He withdrew toward the entrance tunnel. "Beloved, I have difficulty understanding why you yearn after that life when I give you every luxury you could wish for. But I do grasp that your new existence still feels strange to you. Please try to comprehend that I do everything for your good."

"If you say so." She hid her face on her folded arms.

The dragon rummaged in the treasure pile for a moment. "I shall leave you to your thoughts, then." Then she heard him behind her, leaving the cave.

She occupied herself with flipping through some of the colorfully illuminated books until he returned. Although tempted to check the tree again, she couldn't risk his finding her absent. Judging from the position of the sun when she went out to sit on the ledge, he stayed away longer than usual. She wondered where he had gone, surely not hunting again. They needed no more food today.

When he finally reappeared, he carried something in his talons. She watched him glide to a landing. The object turned out to be a basket with its contents wrapped in cloth. "I have brought you a gift," he said. "I hope it will cheer you."

Too curious to bother going inside first, she unfolded the top layer. She could hardly believe the aroma wafting from the package was what it seemed. "It's fresh bread!" She peeked under the cloth. "Two loaves!"

Hurrying into the great hall, she unwrapped the still warm prize. Tucked into the side of the basket she found a smaller, sticky package—a wedge of honeycomb. Her eyes widened with delight. "Oh, Virid, how did you get it?"

Keeping his dragon shape, he curled on the floor like a giant cat. "Easily enough. I scented the hive in a hollow tree and subdued the bees with smoke, as your beekeepers do."

"No, I mean the bread, of course." She spread a cloth on the chest they used as a table and broke off a chunk from a loaf. After the scant amount she'd eaten earlier, her stomach cramped with hunger. She swallowed to keep from drooling.

"I bought it. After all, I have plenty of coins." A smug tone colored his reply.

"What? How—?"

"I took human shape and walked into a town. Not your own, a larger one some distance away."

"But you don't look human," she blurted. How could he walk among ordinary people, with his olive skin and silver-blue crest of hair?

"With a cape and hood, my peculiarities are not obvious."

"What about the risks you keeping harping on?" She smeared honey on the bread and took a generous bite. The flavor warmed her down to her toes.

"I have prudence and skill enough to keep out of sight while in my true form. The folk of the town saw me only in the guise of a cloaked man."

"Well, this is more than wonderful. Would you like some?" She held the fragment of bread up to his grinning jaws.

"No, thank you. I am pleased that you enjoy it. You said you missed bread and honey."

She paused in the act of stuffing another bite into her mouth. "You remembered that?"

"I remember every word you speak. And I would not have you unhappy." His tail and forelegs embraced her.

Savoring the heat he radiated, she turned to hug his neck. "Thank you!" She planted a kiss on his scales. When his tongue whipped out to lap drops of honey from her mouth, she melted inside. Nothing had forced him to bring her this gift. As long as she remained his bedmate and brood mare, he need not have taken any notice of her fretful mood. And regardless of his claims, he had risked attack or capture. He must care for her more than she'd realized.

Contracting into man-shape, he wrapped his arms around her. When he kissed her more deeply, whispered yearning words against her lips and neck, and lapped his way down to her flowing quim, her thoughts scattered and her body dissolved into a flood of delectable sensation.

Despite Virid's kindness, Rowena knew better than to broach the subject of her family again. Even though he had risked his own life in a visit to a human town, he wasn't likely to change his mind about forbidding her to do the same. As soon as she could slip away while he slept that night, she flew to the tree of tribute.

The moment she landed, she noticed moonlight glinting on metal. She swooped down upon the object. Her bronze amulet lay half under a large rock, with parchment tied to it. With her heart pounding, she snatched up the packet. Even dragon eyes couldn't read quill scratchings by this faint light. Rather than trying, she hurried back to the cave with her find.

With Virid asleep, she judged it safe to read her message inside the lair. In woman shape, dressed only in a silk undertunic, she retreated to one of the side alcoves and unfolded the parchment. It was her own letter, she discovered, with a fresh note written on the back in what looked like berry juice. Used to reading by the glow of the walls, she had little trouble deciphering the words.

"Dear Granddaughter: Your mother and father and brothers are well, save for Harold. He has been sick with the fever, and he now has the cough in his chest. We fear he may die. I did not tell anyone of your message. It is not safe. I thank the Blessed Virgin that you live. Your loving Grandmother."

Fever. Cough. So Harold had fallen ill with typhoid and the disease had led to lung fever, as it often did. Rowena buried her face in her hands, tears welling in her eyes. She had to do something, but what? Would the healing potion stored on the medicine shelf cure disease? Perhaps, if only she could deliver it to her brother, something Virid would not allow.

With unshed tears choking her, she burned the message in the dying embers of the fire pit, then huddled on her bed cushions, staring at the ceiling in silent misery. Her hand wandered over her distended stomach, larger by the day, it seemed, with the skin as tight as a drum-head. As long as she carried the dragon's child, he would never let her show herself among people.

Yet she felt she had to ask, at least. Suppose her brother died without her ever seeing him again? At daybreak she confronted Virid, first broaching the other subject that preyed on her mind. "The baby," she said, standing on the ledge in her shift, with gusts of wind molding the cloth to her body. "I've gotten big so fast, but I don't feel quickening."

The dragon spread his claws across her swollen belly. "The child lives. I sense it." When he focused his gaze on the place he touched, the faint glow appeared.

"Then why can't I feel it moving?"

"You ask questions I cannot answer. Centuries have passed since I saw a young wyrmling, and I have never fathered one myself. Thousands of years ago we thronged these lands, but I was only a dragonet myself then. And even before time and human warriors thinned our ranks, we led solitary lives. Unless mated, a dragon lives alone."

"Don't you get lonely?"

He snorted. "A typically human question. We do not need to gather in herds the way your kind do. We mate for life, and a dragon who cannot find his destined beloved prefers solitude. Besides, more than two dragons living at close quarters would quickly strip their land of prey."

"What happens when the baby grows up, then?"

"He must range widely enough to find his own territory. No great task, with so few of us left in this country. But that lies far in the future. We will have many years with our child. Soon enough, he will come forth."

"Or she," Rowena absently corrected. "How soon?"

He said with an impatient flutter of his wings, "You persist in asking for answers I do not have. Almost two months have passed since you conceived. If you were a pure she-dragon, the time would be almost here. But you have human blood. And from all I have heard, these cross-breedings are always shaped by the unpredictability of magic."

She drew a deep breath to nerve herself for what she had to ask.

"If there's no telling when I'll give birth, then I want to see my family now, one last time, before the baby comes."

Tendrils of smoke curled from his nostrils. "I have spoken my final word on that subject."

"Only once, just to let Mamma know I'm alive. I can't let her go through the rest of her life thinking I was torn apart and devoured. And I want to talk with Grandmother and hear the full truth about her dragon. I have to do this, have to know." She couldn't state her real reason, the need to find out how sick Harold was and help him if possible.

"Out of the question!" he roared

Tears burned her eyes. "I'll never ask for such a thing again. I'll follow all your commands without a single protest."

"I have explained why I cannot allow it. Why can you not rest content with all I've given you? Why must you ask for the impossible?"

"It's not impossible!" She planted her hands on her hips, raising her voice to match his shout. "It's just your stubbornness. You're so hardheaded you won't admit I can take care of myself."

"My jewel, the danger —"

"Stop blathering about how it's for my own protection, and stop calling me that. You treat me like part of your treasure hoard instead of a mate."

"Do I have to lock you up like a treasure to keep you from throwing away your life and our child's?"

"Just try it!" She marched into the cave, calling over her shoulder, "You can't watch me every minute. I'll fly away, and you'll never see me again — or your wyrmling."

Following, Virid slithered past her, shimmered, and flowed into human shape. He grasped her by the shoulders and gazed into her eyes. "Do not even speak of such a thing."

She tried to wriggle free of his hands, but he held her too firmly. "Would you keep me here by force? Just as I suspected all along, I'm only a possession or a breeding animal to you."

"No, my dear one!" His eyes gleamed with sadness, not anger, and the pressure of his fingers slackened. "If you fled, I would indeed be — lonely. I have never felt loneliness before, yet I know its meaning. It is the emptiness I would suffer if you left me."

"A likely tale. You'd miss our swiving, you mean." She pulled away from him and stalked over to the chest that held her clothes.

"Yes, of course, but not only that. I could always find another wench for that purpose." He followed her across the chamber, his fists clenching and unclenching at his sides, as if he fought the urge to seize her again. "Rowena, what are you doing?"

With abrupt, jerky movements, she pulled a kirtle out of the box and tied it into a bundle with her shift. "Going out, the way you gave me permission weeks ago, remember?" She took a few strides toward the exit.

"Where?" He stepped into her path.

"Don't worry, I'm not going to the village. I'm not stupid enough to try that in daylight, and you would stop me anyway, wouldn't you?"

"I would not allow you to take that risk with our young," he said, standing stiffly motionless in front of her. "But otherwise I would not use force to confine you."

"Good, because I need to get away from you. Don't follow me."

A shadow of what looked like sadness fell over Virid. Without another word, he retreated to the treasure pile, lay down, and closed his eyes without changing form.

An ache tugged at Rowena's breast, tempting her to run to him and throw her arms around him. Could it be that he would actually suffer if he lost her? She stifled the impulse to offer him comfort. Surely that display of sorrow was only a dragonish trick to get her to surrender to his will. Besides, if his pain was real, let him wallow in it for a while. The experience would teach him a lesson.

Chapter Eight

๛

With her bundle of clothes, she flew to the open meadow where the two of them had frolicked several times. After dressing, she strolled around the field, picking wildflowers and savoring the summer breeze and the coolness of grass underfoot. Or pretending to savor it. Her thoughts kept wandering back to the lair. Hours passed while she alternately walked until she grew tired and dozed beside the stream or bathed her feet in it. Her head pounded with confusion. She had to take that healing potion to her brother, yet she could not openly defy the dragon. And the new fear that she might actually hurt her mate by her defiance added to her turmoil.

When hunger threatened to drive her back to the cave, she shapeshifted and killed a wild goat. In dragon form, she had no qualms about devouring it raw. Finally, when the sun began to sink toward evening, she decided she had punished Virid enough. Not only that, she had worked out a plan to bring aid to her family. *After this one last time,* she resolved, *I shall become the kind of mate he wants.*

Upon her return to the lair, she found Virid, still man-shaped, waiting with a cooked haunch of venison upon a silver tray, a decanter of Burgundy wine, and a spray of wild roses arranged in a Grecian vase. The rest of the bread lay sliced on a platter.

Motionless, he watched her approach and change into woman form. The grave sadness on his face unsettled her. Was he offering a sincere expression of remorse, or was he only trying to appease her and get her under his control? He beckoned to her. "Drink with me, and say you forgive what you call my stubbornness."

She noticed he didn't admit to being wrong, much less offer to let her visit her family. Her plan required her to accept his overture, though. "I don't want to quarrel with you. Let's say no more about it for now."

She put her hand into his. "And I never want to quarrel with you," he said, his voice rough with yearning. Drawing her close, he wrapped his arms around her and gave her a lingering kiss.

With no will of her own, her lips parted to welcome the flicker of his tongue. The familiar honeyed warmth flowed through her veins. Sighing, she settled on the cushions beside him, with his arm draped over her shoulders while he fondled her breast. She nibbled the bread and offered him a bite from her fingertips. He sucked her fingers into his mouth and circled each in turn with his tongue.

Shivering, she pulled her hand away and poured a goblet full of the tart, crimson wine. She took a small sip before handing him the cup. Getting tipsy herself did not enter into her plan. She urged him to drink while she sampled the bread and meat. They fed each other and passed the cup back and forth, his fingers constantly playing with her hair and caressing her nipples. Delectable sensations rippled through her. Lightheaded, she forced herself to keep her mind on her goal.

"This wine makes my mouth pucker," she said, trilling a laugh that she hoped he wouldn't recognize as false. The claim itself, at least, was true. "I want some mead to sweeten my palate." She slipped out of his embrace to pick up another pair of cups and fill them from the mead cask. To her relief, Virid waited for her rather than getting up. In an alcove out of his sight, she emptied an entire vial of poppy extract into his drink. She had to make sure he slept soundly and long this time.

As she walked toward him, he reclined on one elbow, watching her like a starving man gazing upon a banquet. His unguarded need stabbed her with a moment of guilt for her trickery, but she suppressed it. If he'd listened to reason in the first place, she wouldn't have to do this to him. Again she took only tiny sips from her cup. When he didn't drink as freely as she wanted, she held the goblet to his mouth, laughing. "You got me drunk the first time we caroused together, remember? Why shouldn't I be able to do the same to you?"

"Why, so you can ravish me as I lie helpless?" He smiled as if genuinely amused by her game. The sight of his needle-sharp teeth, almost like the fangs of a snake, reminded her of the way they gripped her neck when he ravished her as a dragon. The memory stirred warmth in the pit of her stomach.

"You won't find out unless you cooperate." She offered him the goblet again.

With a low chuckle, he gulped down the rest of the drink. "There, I have obeyed your will, and you have me in your power. A fitting revenge for my taking you captive." He swept her into his arms, and they toppled onto the cushions together. His eyes, fixed on hers, smoldered with the same glow they held when he wore his dragon shape.

He kissed her, titillating her tongue with the sticky sweetness of the mead. Its flavor and the thrill of his touch intoxicated her. *No, I have to stay alert. I mustn't fall into the trap I set for him.*

She broke off the kiss. He nibbled her ear and her neck, making her shiver again. Rising to her elbows, she flicked one of his nipples with her tongue. His moan of pleasure gave her a sense of power that she couldn't help but pause to enjoy.

She slithered down his body, licking along the patterns of his pale, olive-tinged scales. The smoothness of his skin under her caressing hands made her palms tingle. His cock jutted into the air by the time she reached it. Taut veins stood out on the rigid shaft. The engorged, crimson tip almost scorched her lips when she tasted it. She traced the pattern of veins with her tongue until he growled in desperation, then sucked the head into her mouth. His hips bucked. She swirled her tongue around the tip, tasting the salty droplets that oozed from it.

"Now—" he groaned.

Yes, now. She wanted him drained so that he would sleep quickly. She drew more of the shaft into her mouth and laved it with her tongue. His back arched, and his hips pumped at frantic speed. A geyser of hot fluid erupted into her throat. She swallowed over and over until he went limp. His labored breathing filled her ears.

When she lay on her side next to him, his eyelids were drooping. He cupped her rounded belly and ran his hand over it in a lingering caress. "You have consumed me, my jewel," he said, his voice slurred. "I need to rest."

"Yes, we should sleep." She hoped her reply didn't sound too anxious.

She felt heat radiate from him, and his shape began to blur. She sat up just in time as the transformation overcame him. He loomed over her in dragon form.

"You are right. I must sleep. Have you forgiven me?"

"Yes." She wasn't sure how true that was, but she did believe he sincerely craved her forgiveness.

"Beloved." He clamped his claws around her forearm, not quite hard enough to cause pain. "You will not leave me, will you?" His emerald eyes glistened.

Guilt clogged her throat. She rubbed her cheek against the smooth scales of his neck. "Of course not." *Not for long, anyway.*

He nuzzled her one final time, lurched to his bed of gems, and sank into a stupor.

While he lay like a colossal figure carved of stone, she wrapped a fresh undertunic and kirtle with a pair of hose and shoes. Into the bundle she tucked a pouch of copper farthings and halfpennies, modest enough in value that her parents could spend them slowly without drawing suspicion. Last she added one of the two vials of healing potion. Virid would certainly notice the loss of it, unlike the poppy syrup. No matter, she would face his anger when the time came.

Carrying the bundle, she flew through the quiet night to the edge of the forest that bordered the village. There she shifted form and scrambled into the clothes. She had to lace the bodice of the kirtle high above her waist, because of the hard bulge in her stomach. At a brisk walk, she headed for her family's holding. Without the stamina of a dragon, she quickly started panting from exertion. Pebbles on the path, harder than the soft earth of the forest, hurt her feet through the soles of the embroidered slippers that she'd settled for in her hurry. With her human eyes less attuned to the moonlight, she stumbled a few times.

Nobody challenged her on the way. She paused by her grandmother's hedge to catch her breath and press a hand against the stabbing pain in her side. When it faded, she crept to the door. Grandmother would welcome her, she knew. Rowena wanted some preparation before astonishing her parents with a return from certain death. Shaking, she tapped lightly on the door.

An inarticulate grumble interrupted the faint snore from inside. With a nervous glance toward her parents' cottage across the yard, Rowena knocked again.

"Who is it?" came the old woman's voice.

"Please, Grandmother, it's me. Let me in," Rowena answered in a rapid whisper.

"What?"

"Hurry, open the door." She couldn't speak louder, for fear of waking the rest of the family.

Slow steps dragged across the floor inside. Finally, she heard the bolt removed and the latch lifted. Grandmother stood in the doorway, wearing a plain shift, with her gray hair straggling loosely around her shoulders. She looked thinner than Rowena remembered.

"Child, is that really you? Get inside before anybody sees you." She grabbed Rowena's wrist and pulled her into the single room, shutting and bolting the door. "Come, sit down. I can light one candle, and no one should notice with the shutters closed." By the glow of the banked coals in the central hearth, she groped for a tallow candle and lit it from the embers. The stuffy room filled with the odor of melting fat.

Rowena accepted a seat on the one stool by the hearth under the smoke hole in the roof, while Grandmother sank onto the bed. "Why did you dare to come here, girl, in your condition? Suppose anyone catches you? You are with child by the dragon, aren't you?"

"You should know. Your dragon sired your baby, didn't he?"

After a long silence, Grandmother said, "Aye. I let the people here think Robert, my man who died, was the father, but it wasn't so." She got up and filled a cup from a jug on a shelf. "Here, you must need this."

Rowena took a gulp from the mug. Ale, something she hadn't tasted since her capture. "Why did you leave your dragon? Did you escape because he treated you cruelly? Or did he cast you out, the way our neighbors think?"

"Not exactly." Seated on the bed again, Grandmother stared at Rowena's rounded stomach in the candlelight. "Your pregnancy is different from mine. My unborn babe didn't grow that fast. My dragon gave me the choice to leave, and I took it."

"Why? Didn't he want a child?"

"Oh, yes, but his magic showed him early on that my baby would look fully human. He wanted a young dragon to bring up."

"So he threw you out? That sounds cruel to me."

"Not at all." The old woman twisted her fingers together in her lap. "He did not believe a human child would be happy growing up in a dragon's lair. He thought the baby deserved a chance at a normal life. When he put it that way, I agreed."

"So you left. Wandering alone couldn't have been easy."

"No, it's a wonder I wasn't ravished by bandits before Robert took me on as a partner. You know the rest of the tale. We found our way here just before Robert fell sick and died, and your mother was born soon after."

"How long did you carry her?" Rowena touched her tightly rounded abdomen.

Grandmother looked puzzled. "The usual nine months. It is strange that your womb has grown so big already."

Does that mean my baby won't be human? She shrank from pursuing the question. "What about the amulet?"

"The dragon did give it to me for protection, but not exactly like I claimed. In case I ever ran into another of his kind, he said they would recognize it and not harm me. Of course I couldn't tell the folk here that I'd loved a dragon and he'd given me a talisman of protection. So I made up a half-true story of my escape."

"It worked, didn't it?" Rowena said, sipping the ale and savoring its refreshing tang. "They felt sorry enough for you to let you stay, even if they never quite approved of you."

"But they wouldn't let you do the same. You aren't thinking of asking, are you?"

Rowena shook her head. "I know better. I just had to see my family once more. Especially with Harold so sick. Is he—?" She was afraid to ask.

"He still lives, but not for long, we fear."

"I brought something to help him. We have to go wake them up right now." She set down her mug and stood up.

"What do you mean?"

She patted the pouch tied at her waist. "I have a healing potion. Magic. Tomorrow morning might be too late for my brother. You have to go in first and warn them what to expect."

Grandmother's eyes again lingered on Rowena's stomach. "Just seeing you alive will give them a shock. Maybe you'd better not give them the full story first thing." She took her winter cloak from a chest in the corner and draped it over Rowena. "Wear this so your condition doesn't show." She pulled a russet kirtle on over her shift.

The contrast between the drab, coarse fabric and Rowena's finely woven gown, like the odors of the cramped hut with trampled straw on the earthen floor compared to the cool, crisp scents of the dragon's cave, struck her with awareness of what a different life she'd embraced in the past two months. Would she dwell here now even if she could?

She followed her grandmother across the yard to the larger cottage. While Rowena flattened herself against the wattle-and-daub wall out of the direct line of sight, the old woman tapped on the door. After a few knocks, Rowena's father opened it. She stifled a gasp at the sound of his voice.

"We have a visitor," Grandmother said in a quavering whisper. "One who has to be kept secret."

"What are you talking about, Mother Joan?" He sounded none too pleased about being awakened with mysterious news.

"Be quiet, and I'll tell you." She slipped inside. Rowena heard murmurs through the open door but couldn't distinguish words.

Abruptly her father's voice rose to a shout. "What? Are your wits addled?"

A piercing cry from her mother: "Are you sure? It's not her—"

Grandmother cut her off with, "No, it's not her ghost. Your daughter is alive. Now, hush. Do you want to wake the whole town?" She beckoned to Rowena, who clutched the cloak snugly around her to hide the pregnancy and stepped into the doorway. Grandmother hustled her inside, with the straw crackling under their feet, and slammed the door. The smells of the byre to one side of the main room where the goats sheltered in harsh weather, the sweat of too many bodies in the smoky cottage, and the kettle of pease porridge kept warm on the central stone hearth rolled over her.

"Mamma? Papa?" Rowena glanced from one to the other in the wavering light of the single candle her father held. He wore only a pair of breeches, and his straw-colored hair stuck out in all directions.

He peered at her and slowly set the candle down on the rough-planked table. "By Our Lady, it's really you." He didn't smile. "How did you escape?"

"I didn't, exactly. The dragon doesn't keep me chained or locked up. I slipped away, just for tonight, to see Harold."

He frowned. "What do you want with your brother?"

"Joseph," her mother interrupted, "what does it matter how or why she came? We have our child back." Dressed in a hastily donned, unlaced gown, she threw her arms around Rowena, who felt the plump body trembling.

She squeezed her mother in a tight hug. "It's all right, Mamma. I've brought medicine for Harold. A healing potion."

Gently drawing back from the frantic embrace, she noticed her two other brothers, aged six and eight, emerging from the back room. Little Peter rubbed his eyes and stared at her. "Rowena? Where did you come from? Are you an angel now?"

She said with a shaky laugh, "No, I'm alive, and I've come to visit Harold. Is he asleep in the loft?"

Papa still looked dubious, but Mamma clasped Rowena's hand and tugged her into the back room. Her father trailed behind them with the light. "I've got him in our bed where I can watch him. He gets worse every day. We've tried all the herbs for fever, and the priest has anointed him, but nothing works."

By the glimmer of the candle, she saw Harold lying on the single bed in the smaller room, near the ladder that led to the loft where the children normally slept. The little boy's cheeks flushed red, and his open eyes looked dazed. He blinked at the sight of his sister. "R'weena? You're home!" The words triggered a fit of coughing.

Mamma dipped a cloth in a basin of water and wiped his forehead. "He got better for a while, and then the fever came back. It settled in his chest, as you see. And he has blood in his stools." She rubbed her eyes.

Sitting lightly on the edge of the bed, Rowena untied the pouch at her waist and got out the blue vial. "I brought something to make you well, Harold. Will you drink it for me?"

Papa grumbled from behind her, "I have my doubts about this magic."

"Then keep them to yourself," Mamma snapped. "Rowena, give it to him."

Uncorking the vial, Rowena inhaled its fragrance, like honey and roses. "Drink up, Harold, and you'll feel better in no time." She hoped the dragon was right about the virtues of this potion.

"Does it taste nasty?" the boy asked.

"Oh, no, it's delicious," Rowena said, counting on the flavor to match the delightful scent. She slid her arm under his back and raised him to drink from the bottle.

After one sip, Harold gulped down the liquid. "That's the best thing I ever tasted. I feel all warm inside." His voice already sounded less reedy, and he didn't cough after speaking. "Can I have more?"

Rowena laughed softly, lightheaded with relief that the remedy seemed to work. "I'm afraid that's all I have."

"The sickness is leaving him," her mother whispered, her hand against his brow to test the temperature. He's already cooler."

"Too soon to tell," said Papa, but he sounded less suspicious than before.

The brothers crowded into the bedchamber, followed by Grandmother. "He's recovering, isn't he?" the old woman said.

"Yes," said Rowena's mother, "it's a miracle."

Her father put in, "He may be getting well, but I wouldn't call it a miracle." His eyes met Rowena's. "Still, we thank you, daughter."

Her two brothers threw their arms around Rowena, who stood up to hug them. "I'm glad you're back," Peter said. "You can stay now, and it'll be just like before."

Her father gave her a sharp look over their heads. "Time enough to talk about that tomorrow, lads. Say goodnight to your sister and go back to sleep."

"But, Papa—"

"No more of that. Go."

Rowena kissed each of the boys on the forehead and detached their clinging arms. "Goodnight, up you go." She watched them climb the ladder to the loft.

When she looked back at her parents, she found them staring at her, Mamma with open-mouthed amazement and Papa with narrowed eyes. She realized the cloak had fallen open to reveal her swollen stomach.

"What have you done, girl?" he said in a harsh whisper.

"Let's talk in the other room, so the children can sleep," Grandmother said.

Mamma glanced at Harold, already asleep, with the feverish red gone from his cheeks. She drew up the sheet with a final pat. Together they all withdrew to the outer chamber.

Papa sat on the bench at the trestle table like a judge about to pronounce sentence. "Well? What's the meaning of this?"

"Don't badger the girl," Grandmother said, "when you can see for yourself what it means. She did what she had to. If it weren't for the dragon's favor, your son would still be dying."

"I've thanked her for that, and I meant it." He frowned at Rowena. "But it was dangerous for you to come here. If you'd been caught, who knows what might've happened to our family?"

"Well, she wasn't," Mamma said, "and I thank the saints she's here. Child, sit down and have something to eat." She dished up a bowl of pease porridge and unwrapped a loaf of black bread.

Abruptly aware of hunger and weariness, Rowena sank onto the bench and dug into the food. Her mother drew a mug of ale and set it in front of her. "I brought you something else," Rowena said when she'd had a few bites and a long drink. She tilted the pouch onto the table and spilled out a handful of copper coins. "This should last you awhile."

"What is that, dragon's treasure? It's unlucky," Papa said.

Mamma, though, scooped the money into her hand. "Nonsense. It looks like honest coin to me, and if we spend it with care, nobody will question where we got it."

"I can bring you more," Rowena said, "when I come to visit Harold next time."

Her father glowered at her. "What do you mean, next time? You can never come here again."

Chapter Nine

ℬ

Mamma gasped.

"But, Papa—" Rowena's eyes stung.

"I'll hear no more about it. We'd all be in danger if you got caught, not just you. And what if the dragon came after you? He might burn the village to get you back."

"I didn't think of that," her mother said, with a nervous glance toward the bedchamber. "There's the boys to consider."

"Don't worry," Rowena said, swallowing her tears. "I'll be gone before sunrise. I just want to stay long enough to make sure Harold's all right."

To her sorrow, a faint expression of relief flitted over her mother's face.

"That's all right, then," her father said, relaxing. "Just see that you keep away from now on."

"I wouldn't think of putting you in danger," she said. Though she knew he was right, she couldn't help feeling hurt by his eagerness to get rid of her. Perhaps he believed, like the rest of the village, that Grandmother had brought the curse of disease on the community, so that she, Rowena, deserved her fate.

Papa leaned back on the bench to rest against the wall behind him. "If all goes well, we may get free of the dragon by this time next year. Then you can take some of that treasure and go your own way."

"Free? How?"

"Folks say the Baron has a plan so we won't be at that monster's mercy anymore. The wizard's working on enchanted arrows to be ready for the dragon when it comes for next year's tribute."

The dragon would never ask for another maiden, Rowena knew, but she couldn't explain that to her parents.

Grandmother sniffed. "You know what I think of that foolishness."

"Not foolishness, Mother Joan. I heard it from one of the lord's servants last market day. It's a long, slow job, but they claim the wizard boasted it will take only a few hits to kill the beast. Or maybe they'll wound it just enough to make it harmless and drag it in chains to the Baron's keep."

Chilled, Rowena said, "Why would they do that?"

Her father shrugged. "To slice pieces off its living body for the wizard's spells? To drain its venom for potions? Force it to reveal where the treasure's hidden? How should I know? Maybe the Baron wants to kill it slowly so its hide won't be spoiled for making armor for his knights."

The food she'd eaten congealed into a lump in Rowena's stomach. Thank Heaven her father had no idea she was part dragon herself. Furthermore, both he and Virid were right in saying it was too dangerous for her to visit the town. She would leave before daybreak and never return, as she'd promised.

Obviously noticing her sick expression, Mamma squeezed her hand. "Don't trouble yourself about it, child. Finish your supper and rest a while. You have hours yet until dawn."

"I'm not hungry anymore." She took a final sip of ale to settle her stomach. She would have left right away, but weariness dragged her down, and she did want to make sure Harold was cured before she departed.

With her mother, she tiptoed into the other room to check on him. He still slept, breathing easily. "I think he's really well," Mamma said when they returned to the outer chamber. "But I'll tell you if there's any change. You rest here by the fire." After a hug and kiss, her mother left Rowena curled up on the floor, wrapped in the cloak, with her back braced against the raised hearthstones. Her father gave her only a wordless grunt of farewell before joining his wife in the bedchamber. Grandmother huddled on the bench, her eyes half-closed.

Rowena meant to rest but not sleep, partly to make the most of her last night with her family and partly for fear of staying too long. "Tell me one of your tales, Grandmother. A story of Robin Hood and Maid Marian," she said, thinking of her hiding place in the woods and her dream of living as an outlaw. Like Robin and his band, she was an outcast from her home now.

In her quavering voice, the old woman began to sing a ballad of Robin appearing in disguise at the Sheriff's archery tournament. Verse piled upon verse, and the sound trailed off as Rowena's eyelids sagged. When she caught herself dozing, she lifted her head and forced herself to focus on the words of the song. It sounded distant and faint. Her head drooped. Sleep enveloped her.

Pain wrung her guts. Daggers stabbed her from inside out. She stared at the bulge of her belly. The skin cracked open. The flesh split like ripe fruit. Claws ripped a bleeding hole in her body. A gaping, fanged mouth thrust out of the wound.

Rowena screamed and woke.

Clutching her stomach, she glanced wildly around. Her grandmother snored on the bench. Faint, gray light seeped through the shutters. Roosters crowed outside.

Dear God, I've stayed too long! She heaved herself to her feet. Her pregnancy felt even heavier than it had the day before. The roosters' noise didn't necessarily mean the neighbors were stirring, since the wretched birds crowed at the first glint of sunrise, but it certainly meant Rowena had no time to waste.

She shook her grandmother, who sniffled and blinked at her. "Child?"

"I have to leave. Say goodbye to Mamma and the boys for me." Rowena rubbed moisture from her eyes. No time for that now.

Grandmother gave her a quick, hard embrace. "Yes, of course. Hurry. And be well."

Rowena kissed her on the cheek, unbolted the door, and slipped out. She crept along the outside wall of the house, then darted for the gap in the hedge. Chickens cackled and goats bleated at her passage. Cursing them under her breath, she headed for the most direct path out of town. Despite her fear, the fresh air came as a welcome treat after a night in the smoky cottage.

The path she chose skirted the market square and led toward the river. Once she'd followed the river into the countryside, she would be safe from observation and could change into dragon form and fly away. She quickened her pace, finding herself eager for the airy heights of Virid's hillside. She realized that she even missed her mate. What would he do in his wrath when he discovered she'd taken the healing potion and disobeyed his command? Well, she had ways of pacifying him, she reflected with a smile. And if he refused to forgive her, she could survive without him. The thought gave her an unexpected pang.

With a fold of the cloak over her head to hide her face, she crept behind the houses that lined the square, hurrying from one to the other and taking advantage of the predawn shadows next to the walls. Every minute increased the light from the rising sun. She hoped the crowing of the roosters would cover any other sounds that might give her away. The barking of a dog made her heart race. Crouching in the midst of a cottage's kitchen garden, she waited for the animal to calm down.

When she started walking again, the aroma of fresh bread wafted to her nostrils. She was passing behind the bakery, where of course the day's work began before sunrise. She quickened her steps, hoping a brisk pace would convince anyone who happened to glance out that she was a neighbor with good reason to be on the street. Just as she reached the next house and started onto the lane that curved around it, the rear door of the bakery opened, and the baker himself stepped out. She clutched the cloak tighter around her and scurried faster.

"Who's there?" the man called. "Stop—aren't you—?" He dashed over to Rowena, grabbed her by one arm, and pulled the cloth off her head. The cloak fell open, leaving her fully exposed. "It can't be. You're dead!"

"Please," she whispered. "Let me go."

"Not so fast. How did you escape?" From the doorway behind him, his son Will emerged. The boy stopped, dumbfounded, to stare at Rowena. When his eyes settled on her stomach, his face darkened with outrage. The baker glanced over his shoulder and said, "Will, get some of the men here as fast as you can." With a tight grip on Rowena's wrist, he led her into the square.

She fleetingly considered changing into a dragon and flying away, but letting the townspeople know about her inhuman side seemed like a desperate last resort. Maybe she could talk her way out.

A cramp racked her. She doubled over, hand on her abdomen. Blinded by the pain, she stumbled as the baker dragged her along. A minute later, in the center of the village green, she found herself the object of hard stares from three of the aldermen. Will stood among them.

Shaking with anger, he pointed at her. "Devil's whore!"

"Will, please don't!"

"You wouldn't lie with me," he said, "but you've fucked a monster."

She tried to straighten up. "You have no right to say that."

"You can't deny it, slut. The midwife testified to your virginity before the sacrifice, didn't she?"

The baker crossed himself. "That's right, she did. No natural child could grow that big so fast. Will, call the priest."

The boy ran off again. Rowena pulled against the baker's hand on her arm, but she couldn't match his strength. By the time the priest appeared, a handful of other people had gathered to stare at her. "Look at her!" Will shouted. "She's carrying the spawn of the Devil."

"He doesn't know what he's talking about," she said. "Let me go. I've done you no harm." Her face flushed with anger and the effort of fighting the baker's bruising grasp. Another cramp squeezed her stomach. Tears welled in her eyes.

Striding to the center of the green, the priest raised his cross and intoned words in Latin. He uncorked a small bottle and splashed water in her face. Holy water, no doubt. Did he think it would scald her? "I'm no demon, you half-witted—"

A wave of pain swamped the words. She crumpled to her knees, wrenching the arm that the baker still gripped. She felt the change surge over her. Her clothes ripped and fell off. The man let her go with a scream when she swelled into dragon shape.

Fly! she thought. *Now, it's my only chance!* The pain nailed her to the ground, though. She felt as if her vital organs were splitting open.

One final wave, and the agony faded to nothing. Mingled gasps and cries rose from the few people who remained close enough for her to hear. She whipped her head from side to side, glowering at them. They had retreated to the edge of the green. Terrified though they were, she was surprised to find them staring, not directly at her, but at something behind her. She turned to look.

An egg lay on the trampled grass. The size of the hard bulge she had carried in her womb, it had a pearly·shell with a faint, blue-green radiance.

So my child is a dragon after all, she thought. Now, while the spectators stood dumbfounded, would be the moment to snatch up the egg and fly to safety. But she couldn't raise herself from the ground. She was too weak even to unfold her wings to their full span. All she could do was wrap her tail around the egg and glare at the men.

One of the aldermen whispered instructions to Will, who left at a run. The elder then spoke softly to another lad lingering on the fringe of the group, and he, too, trotted away. The priest brandished his cross and resumed his Latin chant in a booming voice. He must have thought his incantations and holy water had drained Rowena's power.

While she struggled to rise to her feet, a couple of the men inched closer, daggers drawn. What they thought their knives could do to a dragon, she had no idea. She roared at them, and they retreated. Probably they expected her to breathe fire. Well, she might have, if she'd had the strength. Sheltering the egg between her claws, she waited. If only she could manage to get off the ground before they built up enough courage to rush her.

Before either event happened, the blacksmith and his apprentice marched into the square. They carried folded lengths of chain.

She roared again, this time in panic. The blacksmith threw a loop over her head and pulled it tightly around her jaws like a muzzle. Seeing that she didn't bite his head off, other men charged in to help bind her legs. She tried to lash her tail at them, but she was still too weak to do more than brush the grass with it. When one of them laid a hand on the egg, though, she raked him with her claws. They left the egg alone after that.

Though she flailed and fought until her energy gave out, with two men holding each leg down, they managed to get her loosely shackled by all four limbs. The blacksmith hammered spikes into the ground to secure the chains in place.

Bowing her head over the egg, through heavy-lidded eyes she watched the priest pour holy water on the wound of the man she had scratched. Now she knew Virid had spoken truth when he said she had to choose between her human life and her new one. The people she'd thought of as her neighbors would never see her as anything but a monster. What did they plan to do with her?

About an hour later by the sun, she found out.

The Baron rode into the village square at the head of a dozen men at arms on foot, all in chain mail. Six swordsmen flanked his steed. The others carried bows. At the rear of the group Rowena glimpsed a man in a monkish robe and cowl. She knew he was no friar, though, but Master Geoffrey, the Baron's household wizard.

The Baron raised an arm. The bowmen formed a half-circle around Rowena, nocked arrows, and prepared to shoot.

"No!" she cried. A few of the villagers in the background flinched. She hadn't spoken in dragon form until now. "Don't

191

hurt me. I only want to leave with my babe." The words came out as a growl, just barely understandable even to her ears.

The wizard spoke up. "Don't listen to the beast's lies, my lord."

"Certainly not. We won't miss this chance to try your enchanted arrows. Strange to find a she-dragon, though. We thought there was only one of the creatures."

"Please, it's only me." With a shudder of effort, she curled around the egg and wrenched her body into human shape. She crouched on the ground naked, with the sun beating down on her back and the loosened chains fallen in a heap around her. "Don't shoot! I'm just Rowena, the maiden you sacrificed."

"So it's true," said the Baron. "The girl did turn into a dragon. I thought that boy was raving." With a lewd chuckle, he added, "Not a maiden anymore, I see. Men, seize her. We'll take her back to the keep and let Master Geoffrey sort this out."

Just as the swordsmen stepped forward, a rush of wind swept over the green. Rowena tilted her head upward. Virid swooped down and landed between her and the Baron's men. She went limp with relief.

He breathed a blast of flame at the nearest swordsman, who collapsed with a shriek of agony. Three of the others turned and fled.

"Stop, you damned cowards!" the Baron bellowed. "I'll have your heads for that. God's blood, shoot it!"

One archer obeyed. The arrow struck Virid on the side of his neck. To Rowena's shock, the point pierced his scales. He roared in pain and shot a gout of fire skyward.

"Enchanted arrows," she whispered.

"You see, my lord, the magic works," the wizard said. More loudly, he called to Virid, "That one didn't kill you, monster, but we have five more. Surrender and let us take you to the castle, and you may be allowed to live awhile."

Ignoring the man, Virid turned to Rowena with anguish in his eyes. He said with a hiss of pain, "Rowenaureadulcima, beloved, take the egg and fly, now!"

"I can't," she gasped. "Too weak."

"Here!" With a talon, he slashed his chest and caught a drop of blood on the tip of his claw. "This will restore your strength." He touched it to her lips, and she automatically licked it off. "Now go!"

She laid her open hand against his smooth-scaled neck. "I can't leave you. They'll kill you." Tears blurred her vision, matching the ones she saw gleaming in his gemlike eyes.

"Never mind that. You must save our child."

The archers were tightening the circle around them. She knew she had to flee, or she and the baby would die, too. Swallowing her tears, she kissed him on the side of his jaw, then pressed her lips to the cut he'd made and tasted another drop of his blood. "Yes—beloved."

Chapter Ten

ဆာ

Energy flooded her. She flowed into dragon form, cradled the egg in her forelegs, and sprang into the air. By the time the bowmen recovered from their astonishment enough to aim their weapons, she had flown too high for an easy shot. A sharp command from the Baron stopped them from wasting arrows. A quick backward glance showed her another shot fired into Virid's leg instead.

She couldn't pause to worry about his fate. She had to keep the egg safe.

Driven by fear and instinct, she fled straight to the lair. As soon as she reached the great hall, she set down her burden and changed to woman shape. She rummaged in a chest for a woolen cloak, which she wrapped around the softly glowing egg. Her legs wobbled, the surge of energy from her mate's blood draining fast. She staggered to the shelves where the potions were stored. One vial of healing elixir remained. She uncorked it and took a small sip.

Piercing sweetness seared through her, burning twice as hot as the liquor she'd imbibed with Virid. The hairs on her arms and legs bristled as if she'd been struck by lightning. She stared at her naked body, almost expecting sparks to dance on her skin. The potion did better than restore the rest of her strength. It made her feel more alive than ever before. Every ache and laceration had disappeared, even the soreness from expelling the egg.

With the physical healing, her head cleared. She realized she needed a different refuge. Suppose the Baron's wizard had discovered the location of the cave? True, the climb to the entrance would be hard, but not impossible for determined men with spikes and ropes. Of course, she could strike them down with her flame breath before they reached the ledge. If Master Geoffrey could enchant arrows to wound a dragon, though, maybe he had some other spell to disable her or at least extinguish her fire. She had to move the egg to a safer place.

After packing a pouch with food, a waterskin filled from the spring, her amulet and the moonstone necklace from the lake as keepsakes, and the vial of healing potion, Rowena shifted to dragon form and gathered up the egg. No one knew about her hideaway in the forest. She could protect her unhatched infant there. Her mate would want the little one cared for above all. Her chest ached at the memory of his swooping down to rescue her. What had the Baron's men done to him? She had no way of finding out now, not until she got their offspring to safety.

Still brimming with energy from the elixir, she quickly flew the distance between the cave and the edge of the woods. There she changed shape to walk among the densely growing trees. She had no trouble finding the clearing with the fallen tree where she had stashed her supplies. The glade had just room enough for her to transform back into a dragon after setting the egg down on the mossy earth. She knew she would have to keep it warm, like a bird's egg, and for that she needed a fire, since she couldn't imagine brooding it in her arms hour after hour.

She cleared a bare space on the ground, then stripped twigs and branches from surrounding trees and stacked them in layers, with dry leaves stuffed among them for kindling. Finally, she started the fire with a puff of flame. She settled the woolen-wrapped egg close enough to get the benefit of the heat but far enough to avoid any risk of burning. Flowing back into woman form, she wondered how long the egg would take to hatch. She'd have to collect fuel to keep the fire going constantly. She thrust aside the other problem nagging at the back of her mind, how to feed a newborn dragon. If only Virid were here to advise her.

At that thought, pain racked her. Now that she had a minute to breathe, she remembered her last sight of the dragon, wounded by a pair of magical arrows. If the wizard had spoken truth, the bowmen had four more in reserve. If they shot Virid in the throat or heart, would he die? Was he dead already?

He had risked his life to save her. She recalled the hurt shadowing his eyes in that moment when he'd gazed at her. Though she had disobeyed his orders and put both herself and the babe in danger, he had shown no anger, only sadness.

True, she'd had to disobey him to heal her brother. She didn't regret that act. But she could have behaved more prudently, departed right after dosing Harold or perhaps even left the vial with her grandmother. Her capture was her own fault, and now the dragon would die for her folly.

Not if I can get to him fast enough.

Making sure the fire was burning steadily and the egg was safe, she hurried through the woods to the open meadow where she had enough space to transform. She launched herself into the air and flew at top speed toward the village. She soared high enough to stay out of range of any arrows from the Baron's bowmen.

When she got within sight of town, she discovered Virid was no longer within its bounds. Instead, the men at arms were dragging him along the road toward the Baron's keep. He must be in a stupor from the magic arrows, she decided, for they pulled him in chains like a dead weight.

Or is he truly dead? At the thought, pain and rage flooded her. A crimson fog veiled her sight. She hurtled toward the ground. The Baron, riding at the head of the procession, looked up and gaped in astonishment. She blasted him with her flames. His clothes ignited like a torch, and his horse screamed and fell onto its side, pinning him under its flank.

The men on foot dropped the chains and scattered. Rowena spared a few seconds to breathe fire in two different directions, catching three or four of the panicked fugitives. The odor of charred flesh choked her.

Descending the rest of the way and folding her wings, she alighted beside Virid. Thanks to the saints, his eyes opened and met hers. "Rowenaureadulcima?" He spoke her dragon name in a harsh whisper instead of a booming roar.

She flicked his neck with her tongue. "Now you have to fly. Hurry, they might work up the nerve to come back!"

"Cannot," he rasped.

"Then change to a man so I can carry you."

"Too weak. The arrows. Go, my love. Cannot let you die, too."

Dragon tears scalded her eyes. "Listen to me, Viridiseffulgentissimus! I won't let you die." She remembered what he had done for her on the village green. Gouging her own neck with a claw, she forced her mate's mouth to the scratch. She felt his hot, whip-like tongue licking the blood. A shudder of pleasure went through her, despite her fear for him.

A tremor racked his body. With a shivering moan, he turned into a man. When he changed, the chains dropped off, and the arrows embedded in his flesh fell out, but the punctures still bled. He had to cling to Rowena to keep from collapsing.

She scooped him up with her forelegs and leaped into the sky. A few minutes later, she landed at the verge of the forest. "I can't fly into the trees," she said, "so I have to turn back to human." After gently placing him on the ground, she changed form.

Virid lay on his back, gazing up at her through half-closed eyes. She slid an arm under his shoulders and eased him into a reclining position. "You have to walk. I can't carry you this way."

With a small negative motion of his head, he said, "Cannot walk. Too weak. Beloved, it is no use. I am dying from the poison in my veins. Only a matter of time."

"What kind of speech is that, from a dragon? Your ancestors would be ashamed of you."

His breath rasped with effort. "If we had the healing potion—"

"You don't have to die. I do have the potion, hidden in the woods." She could go fetch it, except that she was afraid to leave him. What if he succumbed to the deadly magic before she got back? What if a wild beast wandered by or one of the Baron's men stumbled upon him? "Up! All you have to do is walk with me a short way."

"You brought the potion? Well done. Then I shall try." Leaning on her, he struggled to his feet. For a few seconds they stood face to face, clinging to each other, his body slick with blood against her bare skin. Their lips met in a gentle kiss. His normally hot, dry flesh felt clammy and chilled.

"This way." She draped his arm around her shoulders and staggered when he rested most of his weight on her. One step at a time, they shuffled into the forest. Her nerves twanged with anxiety at the slowness of their progress. She practically had to drag him.

At last they reached her clearing. "You saved our child," he said in a barely audible whisper when he saw the egg beside the fire. "You are indeed a precious treasure, my golden one."

Rowena settled him on the ground and dug the vial out of her pack. Virid's eyes were closed again when she turned back to him. "Wake up!" She smoothed his silver-blue crest of hair and held the potion to his mouth. "Don't frighten me like that. Here, drink it, all of it."

He obeyed, pausing after the first sip to take the vial from her and hold it by himself. Halfway through, his eyes gleamed, and she felt the warmth returning to his flesh. When he finished the elixir, he wrapped one arm around her and cupped her head with his other hand, drawing her close for a long kiss, his tongue teasing the corners of her lips. The hot, spicy taste of his mouth confirmed his healing.

She slipped out of his embrace to get a cloth and soak it in cool water from her waterskin. She wiped the blood from his skin, noticing that the wounds had vanished, and dried him with another piece of linen.

"You tricked me," he said. "You broke your vow." His voice conveyed hurt rather than anger.

"I'm truly sorry." Would he not want her anymore, now that she'd betrayed him? "But I couldn't let my brother die."

"I begin to understand that now. Family bonds have great importance for humankind." He sat up against a tree trunk. "You might have died, though, and our young one with you."

"I know. I should have left right after I gave them the potion, and this wouldn't have happened." She sat next to him, and he put an arm around her.

"When I woke and found you missing," he said, "I thought I had lost you forever. I thought you had chosen your human family, regardless of the risk."

"Oh, no! I always meant to come back to you."

"Are you certain? If you had been so determined to leave me, I would not have restrained you."

"Really?" She stared into his glittering eyes. "You'd have let me go?"

"If your happiness required it."

"I realize now that I couldn't possibly live in the village. They'd never accept me. Even my father—" She choked down the beginning of a sob.

Virid stroked her hair. "You could find another home among human folk, as your grandmother did. Clearly you have the wit to survive."

Did he want her to go away? Or was he simply offering the freedom she had begged for? A shimmer in the corner of her eye interrupted her thoughts. Turning toward it, she realized the egg was glowing brighter, its light rippling like wavelets on a pond. "Look!" She pointed.

Virid stood up. "It is ready to hatch." Even as he spoke, the egg quivered. Both of them stepped closer to watch. A thin crack appeared in the shell. It gradually lengthened, and the inner light pulsed.

"Should we help?" Rowena whispered.

"Not yet. I have never seen birds help their chicks hatch. I believe he needs to build up his strength."

She sank to her knees at arm's length from the egg and watched the crack grow wider. Quietly, Virid crouched beside her, his warm hand on her shoulder. A cluster of tiny claws poked through the gap. She held her breath.

Fragments of shell flaked away. "Now you can break the rest of it," said Virid.

As she peeled off bits, the glow faded. She tore at the inner membrane, through which she glimpsed a wiggling, four-limbed figure. Hooking her fingers into the jagged edges, she ripped the remaining shell in half.

A baby lay in a piece of eggshell as if in a cradle. A human infant, not a wyrmling. Her hands shaking, Rowena wiped away sticky fluid with a corner of the cloak in which the egg had been wrapped. As soon as she cleared the nose and mouth, the baby wailed. She gathered him — Virid had guessed right about the sex — into her arms, swaddling him in the dry part of the cloak. Her chest ached from the warmth of the small body.

Cuddled against her breast, the baby stopped crying and opened his eyes wide. He didn't look fully human, after all. He had emerald, cat-shaped eyes like his father's. His skin had the olive-green hue of Virid's human form, with a pattern of tiny scales. Instead of ordinary nails, he had miniature claws on his fingers and toes. His downy, silver hair grew in a crest pattern. Rowena thankfully noticed that he had no teeth. She wouldn't have cared for the idea of nursing an infant with fangs.

"Perfect," Virid breathed.

She glanced over her shoulder at his fascinated gaze. "You don't mind that he wasn't born a dragon?"

"He has your nature as well as mine, my treasure. How could I not rejoice in that?"

The baby's head turned toward her breast, his mouth rooting with muffled whimpers. Her breasts felt heavy and tingly. She guided a nipple between his lips. He clamped on and immediately began to suck. She gasped at the voracious tug that sent a pang from her nipples to the pit of her stomach.

Virid's hand massaged the center of her back. "Once he has been fed, we must make our plans. I cannot stay in the cave any longer. You did not kill the wizard, did you?"

Thinking back over the moments of rage when she'd rescued Virid, she recalled a glimpse out of the corner of her eye. The wizard, at the fringe of the group, had fled unscathed. "No, and I wish I had. Does that make me evil?"

Virid shrugged. "Good and evil are human ideas. All it means to me is that the Baron's heir may seek revenge, and he may order the wizard to use magic to seek out my lair and destroy me."

Chilled by the realization that her attack on the Baron and his men hadn't ensured the safety of her mate and child, Rowena said, "What can you do?"

"It is no great catastrophe. I have another lair already chosen half a day's flight away, in a more remote location. No dragon would live without such a refuge in reserve. Later I can move my possessions little by little, whatever I do not wish to abandon."

"Wait—you keep saying *I*. You talk as if you're going alone."

"Do you not wish to seek a home among your own kind?"

Her heart racing with the turmoil of her thoughts, she turned her head to stare into his eyes. "You want me to go away?"

"No, never!" His hand covered one of hers, cradling the baby's head along with her. "But I will not hold you captive against your will. All I ask is that you teach our son the truth of his heritage and perhaps allow me to visit him sometimes."

Her chest tightened in sympathy with the anguish in his tone. He would let her go, taking his much-desired offspring with her, just to ensure her happiness? A lump welled in her throat. She swallowed it and fought to keep her voice steady. "I don't want to leave. I never intended that. I love you."

Hope flared in his eyes. "Truly?"

"Oh, yes!" She leaned against him, basking in his heat.

"As I love you." He drew her into a tight embrace, with their child between them, and she twined one arm around his neck. She felt his heartbeat pounding in harmony with hers. Dragon or man, he was her destined mate. Dragon or woman, she belonged to him. Forever.

Why an electronic book?

We live in the Information Age—an exciting time in the history of human civilization in which technology rules supreme and continues to progress in leaps and bounds every minute of every hour of every day. For a multitude of reasons, more and more avid literary fans are opting to purchase e-books instead of paperbacks. The question to those not yet initiated to the world of electronic reading is simply: *why?*

1. *Price.* An electronic title at Ellora's Cave Publishing and Cerridwen Press runs anywhere from 40-75% less than the cover price of the <u>exact same title</u> in paperback format. Why? Cold mathematics. It is less expensive to publish an e-book than it is to publish a paperback, so the savings are passed along to the consumer.

2. *Space.* Running out of room to house your paperback books? That is one worry you will never have with electronic novels. For a low one-time cost, you can purchase a handheld computer designed specifically for e-reading purposes. Many e-readers are larger than the average handheld, giving you plenty of screen room. Better yet, hundreds of titles can be stored within your new library—a single microchip. (Please note that Ellora's Cave and Cerridwen Press does not endorse any specific brands. You can check our website at www.ellorascave.com or

www.cerridwenpress.com for customer recommendations we make available to new consumers.)

3. *Mobility.* Because your new library now consists of only a microchip, your entire cache of books can be taken with you wherever you go.

4. *Personal preferences are accounted for.* Are the words you are currently reading too small? Too large? Too...**ANNOYING**? Paperback books cannot be modified according to personal preferences, but e-books can.

5. *Instant gratification.* Is it the middle of the night and all the bookstores are closed? Are you tired of waiting days—sometimes weeks—for online and offline bookstores to ship the novels you bought? Ellora's Cave Publishing sells instantaneous downloads 24 hours a day, 7 days a week, 365 days a year. Our e-book delivery system is 100% automated, meaning your order is filled as soon as you pay for it.

Those are a few of the top reasons why electronic novels are displacing paperbacks for many an avid reader. As always, Ellora's Cave and Cerridwen Press welcomes your questions and comments. We invite you to email us at service@ellorascave.com, service@cerridwenpress.com or write to us directly at: 1056 Home Ave. Akron OH 44310-3502.